L2

O
Outlines

TALLULAH
BANKHEAD

GW00503255

Other works by Bryony Lavery

Bryony Lavery: Plays One
(London: Methuen)

New Connections: Plays
(London: Faber & Faber)

The Wild Bunch & Other Plays
(Surrey: Nelson)

Masks & Faces
(London: Macmillan)

It Isn't Over Until The Fat Lady Sings
(London: Bodley Head)

Calling The Shots ed. Susan Todd
(London: Faber & Faber)

Manuscripts of Bryony Lavery's are available from:

Peters, Fraser & Dunlop
503/4 The Chambers, Chelsea Harbour
London, SW10 0XF

Outlines

TALLULAH BANKHEAD

BRYONY LAVERY

Absolute Press

First published in 1999 by Absolute Press
Scarborough House, 29 James Street West,
Bath, Somerset, England BA1 2BT
Tel: 01225 316013 Fax: 01225 445836
email sales@absolutepress.demon.co.uk

Distributed in the United States of America and Canada by
Stewart, Tabori and Chang
115 West 18th Street, New York, NY 10011

© Bryony Lavery 1999

The rights of Bryony Lavery to be identified as author of this
work have been asserted by her in accordance with the
Copyright Designs and Patents Act 1988

Series editor Nick Drake

Cover and text design by Ian Middleton

Cover printed by Devenish and Co. Bath

ISBN 1 899791 42 6

No part of this publication may be reproduced, stored in a
retrieval system or transmitted in any form or by any means
electronic, mechanical, photocopying. recording or
otherwise without the prior permission of Absolute Press.

Contents

You go to my head,
and you linger like a glass of champagne ...   7

A Gone With The Wind start   15

Unstable trinitrotoluene   29

The four horsewomen of the Algonquin   45

We have escaped by the luckiest chance ...   59

Beautiful, wild, wilful and wearily discontented   73

Work, work, work, fuck, fuck, fuck   89

Barged down the Nile and sank   99

What art!   109

Girlfriend, district attorney and Driving Miss Daisy   123

Curtain   137

Acknowledgments   143

Filmography   144

A YOUNG TALLULAH BANKHEAD

You go to my head, and you linger like a glass of champagne ...

Scene:	TOTAL DARKNESS. WE HEAR THE STEADY CLACKING OF AN OLD TYPEWRITER. IT STOPS. A VOICE IS HEARD ...
The writer:	*A heavenly light shines on my A4 typing paper ...* *A character begins to form ...* *'Oh Goddess' I whisper ... 'Help me ... help us'* *I light my two hundred and thirty-fourth cigarette.* *I start to write ...*[1]

Call me Shallow, call me Surface (and don't call me before ten in the morning) but what I want to write about are badly-behaved, heavy-drinking, drug-taking, sexy women who have a snappy line in repartee. Not Marie Curie, who worked long and diligently to discover radium to save us from cancer. Not Emmeline Pankhurst, who got us Women's Suffrage. Not Eleanor Roosevelt, Harriet Tubman, Mary Seacole, Nurse Edith Cavell, Violette Szabo, Aung San Suu Kyi, Mother Theresa, Hildegard of Bingen, Boudicca, Hilary Clinton, Kate Millett, Sojourner Truth, Mary Wollestonecraft or those three Bronte women. All Women, all Worthy, Wonderful and Workpersonlike, but – and I know it is because they were working too hard on mine and humanity's behalf to be so – Not Funny.

Hence Tallulah Bankhead. I am a playwright. I work with actors. I like them, particularly the ones who make me laugh. Hence Tallulah Bankhead.

She was no Dame Edith Evans. She was a popular film, stage and radio actress. But not a great one. She appeared in many, many mostly awful, forgettable plays, which were box office successes because she enjoyed lobbing in outrageous asides, performing adhoc cartwheels to show off her gorgeous underwear and playing to the gallery, where sat and whooped her largely gay female audience.

She was no Mother Theresa.

She bragged about having over 500 affairs with both men and women. At her peak, she consumed two bottles of bourbon and 100 cigarettes a day, plus innumerable Class A and B drugs.

She was no Eleanor Roosevelt.

She hated racial and sexual prejudice, wrote a pamphlet 'Human Suffering Has Nothing To Do With Creed, Race or Politics' and helped in getting both Harry S. Truman and John F. Kennedy into the White House.

She was someone who said: 'I've tried several varieties of sex. The conventional position makes me claustrophobic and the others either give me a stiff neck or lock-jaw.'

Whose attitude to seriousness in politics was: 'Jack's [Kennedy] murder was one of the two most horrid moments of my life. The other was when I found out there was no Santa Claus.'

Whose last words were: 'Codeine. Bourbon.'

She *was* Essence of Bad Behaviour. She was Very Funny. She was Impossible.

Here's how I was the first time I came across her. In my childhood, meals, comfort, guidance and one or two smacks were provided downstairs, while upstairs, imagination ran amok. It was a happy, workable arrangement, to stretch an analogy, it was like writing should be. Meanwhile school taught

Beginner's Reality, Intermediate Boundaries and Advanced Narrow Thinking.

'School said that Clever Girls became nurses, teachers or worked in offices. Oh, and incidentally, ran homes too. They did not become nuns, vets, comediennes, artists, detectives, lifeguards and they certainly did not work on trawlers. And I know that was back in the sixties, but when I was a teacher [dear Reader, I did what School taught me], the girls told me at eleven that they were going to be airline pilots, army captains, cartoon artists, and at sixteen left to become shop assistants, hairdressers and to work in offices.'[2]

'Can't and Don't ruled everywhere except in the upstairs of our houses.'[3]

I was looking for the places where imagination ran amok.

First came her name. I thought Tallulah Bankhead was a very funny name. A joke in itself. In line with my great aunt's friend Ida Vickermans who went off and married a Mr Downs. Like a girl at my college called, gloriously, Coralie Fishpool, who met, in her very first term, Jeff Seagrave and, dear Reader, married him. There is a line in Salinger's *Franny and Zooie* where Franny is in transports over the name Dean Sheeter. And my cousin and I were in tucks over WPC Evelyn Hall, who lives on Letsby Avenue. Wolfs, Torfinns, Winks, Canarys, Lallas, Bryonys all get mercilessly teased in the schoolyard, then they get proud of their dumb names, because they get remembered. From little acorns ... Your first meeting in those early years means that hundreds of years later you are engaged in this strangely-intimate relationship of biography but Tallulah is the one who goes out and does everything, I am the dim bulb who sits at home and writes about her.

Skimming the Internet, I find that Bankhead is today also 'the name of a female-fronted band playing punk-inspired pop tunes (or pop-inspired punk tunes) with a little ska and funk thrown in for good measure.' You somehow know there are never going to be bands named after Thorndike, Ashcroft, Flora Robson or Edith Evans.

Noticing Tallulah was the tip of a Titanic iceberg which was going to sink my chances of a normal life because, dear Reader, I was falling in love with words. With words that made jokes. And with people who could throw up handfuls of bright words and juggle them dexterously into a construction that could make me smile (good), laugh (even better), or cry with laughter (paradise, paradise, paradise). Even before I knew anything about sexuality or life, I knew I liked funny women (in *every* interpretation of the word 'funny').

I grew up in the 'Women Don't Have A Sense Of Humour' era. So Dorothy Parker, Bea Lillie, Betty Marsden, Beryl Reid were like far-apart oases in a desert full of the sand of Male Comics.

Sunday lunchtimes, when *Round The Horne* was on the wireless, we would listen *en famille*, mother and father in *their* chairs, children lying in a row, flat on our backs on the carpet. Funny names moved me into a whole new dangerous area of funny words: I would find *Round The Horne's* camp, theatrical characters – Fiona and Charles, aka Dame Celia Molestrangler and Ageing Juvenile Binkie Huckaback – very, very funny indeed. Chou en Ginsberg MA (failed), geisha Lotus Blossom 'played in the manner of a depressed Derek Jameson by Hugh Paddick' and 'not all she's clacked up to be'. Lady Beatrice Counterblast (nee Clissold), whose catchphrase was 'Many, many times. Many, many times'. Then the two ditsy queens, Julian and Sandy, with their strange language 'polare', with its vocabulary 'palare, bona, vada, omi, palone, omipalone, lallies, fantabulosa, troll ... ' and, most glorious of all, Rambling Syd Rumpo with his lyrics (sung to the tune of Waltzing Matilda):

> Once long ago in the shade of a goolie bush
> Toasting his splod by the old faggots gleam
> Reasted a gander man nobbling his woggle iron
> And stuffing a sheep in the old mill stream ... [4]

And disparate words mashed together: Sir Jodrell Fitzloosely, Madame Osiris Gnomeclencher (an astrologist), Queen Gruntfuttock The Terrible, Zsa Zsa Poltergeist, Lady Voleharvest, Mrs Beethoven, Ghengis Khan, Mrs Ivan The Terrible, Mrs Gugielmo Marconi, Betty Marsden's string of parts, Daphne

Whitethigh (her advice: 'How to avoid crow's feet – don't sleep in trees'). Beryl Reid's chipper, Brummie schoolgirl Monica used to have me howling on the living room floor, without me ever considering why I liked them so much. I had a quick-witted mother, sister, aunts, friends, a family of beezer raconteuses. Funny Women were by and large *Amateuses*.

I was finding 'rude' funny before I knew what 'rude' involved. I knew it was about sex, although I didn't know what sex was. I didn't know I was listening to camp, that the language of 'polare, vada, lallies ... ', was the hidden argot of the *love that dares not speak its name*. I just knew it made me laugh. It was about silly, glib, outrageous, theatrical, glamorous fools – and I loved it.

And then I went International. I came across other Amusing Talkers; Dorothy Parker, Mae West, Beatrice Lillie, Betty Macdonald, Judy Holliday, Claudette Colbert, and learned that old Funny-Name Bankhead belonged among them. She had funny things to say. Writers are very slow on the witty riposte, the quick killer comeback, the *coup de grâce* put down. That's why they become writers, to practice and make them up for the next time and that's why they are attracted to those who can. Hence Tallulah.

I had contracted some life-threatening Chronic Conditions. I had a susceptibility to Theatre. Movies. Camp. Homosexuality. Funny Women.

And this is what we have with Tallulah Bankhead:

> '*She was nowhere near a great actress, though once in a while she could be a surprisingly good one. And now all the truths had to be set down, given back, added up – even if, on the whole, they added up to an image of a failure, of fabulous waste. I don't think we expected to see her give a good performance. I think we expected to meet her someday. Really meet her. In person. I think she was too real to us to be good in most parts. She lacked camouflage. There was no chameleon in her.*'[5]

Robin Archer, in her stage show *A Star Is Torn* and her book of the idea behind the show, lovingly points out how those 'Didn't Quite Cut It With

Real Life Girls' – Marilyn Monroe, Billie Holliday, Janice – actually survived awful, difficult childhoods, chipped out incredible carvings of careers from a granite-face of prejudice, homophobia, misogyny and class, and lived lives of incredible, fragile courage. Tallulah belongs with them.

Cecil Beaton pictured her thus:

> *'Tallulah is a wicked archangel, with her flaming ash-blonde hair and carven features. Her profile is perfectly Grecian. She is a Medusa, very exotic, with a glorious skull, high pumice-stone cheekbones and a broad brow. Her cheeks are huge acid peonies. Her eyelashes are built out with hot liquid paint to look like burnt matches. Her sullen, discontented rosebud of a mouth is painted the brightest scarlet and is as shiny as Tiptree's strawberry jam.'*

With Tallulah, we are not going to discover radium, save street beggars, effect social reform, plumb the depths of dramatic tragedy, soar the heights of dramatic interpretation. With Tallulah, we are going to have Fun. John Osborne said his plays were 'lessons in the emotions'. Tallulah's lifestyle is a lesson in party-going. As Mae West said, 'She's the kind of girl who climbed the ladder of success wrong by wrong.'

Smoking, drinking, fucking, drugging up, roaring with laughter from the pages of this book is Tallulah Bankhead. When you have your quiet dull days, with no energy for doing anything but sitting watching Barbara Streisand videos on your sofa, she's your woman. She will be THE BAD GIRL for you; She had the energy, commitment and Braggadocio to behave badly in public and fuck famous faces, female and male.

I am adding her to the collection of wonderful, hilarious, tiresome, insecure, gifted, life-cheering, experience-enhancing female actors I have in my life. The others, I learned about in rehearsal coffee-breaks, on trains returning from tours to the rest of Great Britain, in theatre bars and at late-night meals in Indian restaurants after shows. Tallulah, I have to imagine.

Here is her story.

WILLIAM BROCKMAN BANKHEAD WITH DAUGHTERS TALLULAH (LEFT)
AND EUGENIA

A Gone With The Wind start

Marguerita: *This house here is full of pain.*
                I feel it in my heart.
                Oh — the ache.[6]

Our heroine is born in Alabama on 31 January 1903. 1903, like all years, is packed with incident. The suffragette movement begins in Great Britain. The electrocardiograph is patented. Henry James has just published *The Ambassadors.* Chekhov gets his first production of *The Cherry Orchard.* Picasso is in his 'Blue Period'. Antoni Gaudi starts work on 'La Sagrada Familia' in Barcelona. Schoenberg has just composed *Pelleas et Melisande.* Charles Reed and Allen Stern start building Grand Central Station in readiness for Elizabeth Smart to Sit Down and Weep by it. The early silent feature film, *The Great Train Robbery* plays. Marie Curie discovers radium. The first motor taxi cab tools about London's streets. The first Tour de France bicycle race is won in France by Maurice Garni, an Italian chimney sweep. The US World Series Baseball competition starts and is won by The Boston Red Sox.

The number of paupers receiving relief in London is at an all time high of 73,608. Europe is politically unstable. The Turks, exacting revenge in the Balkans, ruin 200 villages, burn 12,000 houses, outrage 3,000 women, slay 4,700 inhabitants and leave 71,000 people without a roof over their heads. Pogroms are encouraged in Russia, in Kishiney and Gornel. The first garden city is founded in Letchworth, England. Roosevelt receives greetings by wireless telegraphy from Edward VII of England. In Chicago, 600 people die in a theatre when fire breaks out and the fire-proof curtain jams halfway down. On December 17th in Kitty Hawk, North Carolina, Orville and Wilbur Wright fit a 12 horse-power engine to one of their gliders and fly in the air for forty yards, thus accomplishing the first ever aero flight. Its formidable consequences on the century ahead and on our story here are as yet unforeseen.

In Russia, there is murmuring dissent against the Tsar. In Belgrade, King Alexander and Queen Draga of Serbia are murdered, their naked and mutilated bodies thrown out of the windows of their palace. *Vesti La Giunbbe* (on with the motley), by Enrico Caruso, becomes the first ever million-selling record. Our extraordinary, busy, changeable century, which hurtles to its close as I write this, is still in its infancy.

Tallulah Bankhead's folks are Deep-Fried Southern Folks. This comes from her father's 'impressions of Washington' diary of 1893:

> *'One thing that tested my patience on the cars was the sight of white young men giving up their seats to the aromatic coloured ladies: "Judgement thou art fled to brutish beasts". By nine o'clock the throughfares are jammed with a heterogeneous conglomeration of coons. Big niggers, little niggers, fat and attenuated dudes and raggy muffins, belles and despised ones, aristocratic 16th Street niggers, and the more unpretentious, but nevertheless loud smelling South Washington coon, the barber and shoe black, the washed and the unwashed, the latter predominantly. There they are! Behold them in their pride and conceit! Harriet B. Stowe, how do you like your incubated proselytes of freedom?'*

As we can see from this deeply considered and finely thought admission, the heinous crime of blacks – apart from them being unacceptably big, little, fat or thin was that 'they were'.

But then, Daddy was born as Native Americans, trying to hold onto their lands and civilisation, killed General Custer at Little Big Horn.

Astrologically-speaking, Tallulah is not born on the cusp. In Western astrology, she's a freedom loving Aquarian, in Chinese astrology, she's born in The Year Of The Cat. Other Cats are Queen Victoria, Rudolph Nuryev, Cary Grant, Frank Sinatra, Ingrid Bergman, Trotsky, George Orwell, and Doctor Spock – oh and Idi Amin. Cat Ladies 'adore bright and lively company, spend a lot of time on their often extremely beautiful hair, prefer to live alone rather than marry for the sake of it, but, without someone to fuss over, may become a little melancholic. They are not generally profound creatures and disasters of every kind send a Cat shinning up the nearest tree.'[7] Remember the siamese cats in Disney's *Lady And The Tramp*? They are two Tallulahs. While as an owner you are legally responsible for all other animals, you are exempt from responsibility for a cat. You just can't train them. That's Tallulah.

The Aquarian 'lives on a rainbow. What's more, she's taken it apart and examined it, piece by piece, colour by colour, and she still believes in it. Freedom-loving, acutely funny, perverse, original, conceited and independent, she can also be diplomatic, gentle, sympathetic and timid, a curious mixture of cold practicality and eccentric instability, she seems to have an instinctive empathy with the mentally-disturbed.'[8] She's clearly got to get into the entertainment industry!

Her parents are something out of an unwritten Scott Fitzgerald novel. Her father, William Brockman Bankhead, Alabama born, the only son of a cotton-miller, has studied law at Georgetown and is practising in Huntsville, Alabama. He is blonde, blue-eyed and with a body worked-out from captaining the college football team. He wants to get into politics. He's to die for – if you're not after brains, sobriety, steadiness and a conviction that all men and women are created equal.

As autumn 1899 turns the leaves to red and gold, Adelaide Eugenia Sledge, of Virginia, blows into town to buy her trousseau. She has lost her mother shortly after her birth, but, brought up by her father, the son of a Southern planter, and a slew of governesses and nannies is – well, the term 'spoilt brat' springs to mind. Her family are noted for breeding Sledge Hammers: top, fierce-fighting cocks. She has something of their quality: preened, beautiful and highly-bred with a beady eye, on the look out for anything strutting and male. She and Mister Gorgeous meet and it's bells, fireworks, cannons and love at first sight. She breaks her engagement and with it her fiancé's, her mother's and her father's heart, and runs off to Memphis, where they ecstatically marry on 31 January 1900.

Do they live happily ever after? Alas, no.

Eugenia, their first daughter, was born on 24 January 1901. She was the apple of Daddy's eye. She was not a robust child, and they carry her about on a satin pillow. Ada was a delicate bloom of a young mother. Will seemed to run the marriage on the premise that his gorgeous wife should be protected 'from getting too ruffled'. But this does not stop him impregnating her while she is still nursing Eugenia.

On the night of her parents' third wedding anniversary, 31 January 1903, Tallulah Brockman Bankhead was born. Tallulah was named after her grandmother, who family lore tells us was conceived at Tallulah Falls, Georgia, on a move from South Carolina to Alabama. Tallulah Falls is something our Tallulah will embrace as a Life Choice hereafter.

There are a lot of good stories about the name 'Tallulah'. Tallulah Falls is named after the reputed Indian Princess of the waterfall. Tallulah means 'delightful sound' in Choctaw and 'terrible waters' in Chicasaw. Southern women were often called after beauty spots and places of geographical interest, so an earlier stop on that fateful journey would probably have had her as 'Magee' or 'Crystal Springs', a later stop-over as 'Yazoo' or 'Big Black'. As someone conceived at Lupset, Wakefield I think the two Tallulahs got away quite lightly. While Tallulah always averred 'Well, darling, we are the only two scenic wonders in all America' she had a great fondness for the loopy etymology of a besotted, poetic fan who proved to her conclusively that Tallulah was gaelic for 'colleen', as Scots had settled in the South aeons ago – although quite *why* they didn't go for *Colleen Falls*, history draws a veil.

It doesn't matter. What is important is that she is named after her grandmother. This will prove important as her mother Ada falls ill with blood poisoning and dies. She is christened beside her mother's open coffin and then the two little babies are taken in by their grandparents in Fayette.

As she lay dying, Ada wrote in her bible for her newborn daughter:

'As a spiritual source at the end of each exacting day, may I recommend to you, your mother's favourite, the 103rd Psalm.'

This is it. It is beautiful.

'Praise the Lord, O my soul: and all that is within me praise his holy Name. Praise the Lord, O my soul: and forget not all his benefits; Who forgiveth all thy sin: and healeth all thy infirmities;
Who saveth thy life from destruction: and crowneth thee with mercy and loving kindness; Who satisfyeth thy mouth with good things: making thee young and lusty as an eagle.
The Lord executeth righteousness and judgement: for all them that are oppressed with wrong.
He shewed his ways unto Moses: his works onto the children of Israel.
The Lord is full of compassion and mercy: long-suffering and of great goodness.
He will not alway be chiding: neither keepeth he his anger for ever.
He hath not dealt with us after our sins: nor rewarded us according to our wickednesses.
For look how high the heaven is in comparison of the earth: so great is his mercy also toward them that fear him.
Look how wide also the east is from the west: so far hath he set our sins from us.
Yea, like as a father pitieth his own children: even so is the Lord merciful unto them that fear him.
For he knoweth whereof we are made: he remembereth that we are but dust.
The days of a man are but as grass: for he flourisheth as a flower of the field.
For as soon as the wind goeth over it, it is gone: and the place thereof shall know it no more.
But the merciful goodness of the Lord endureth for ever and ever upon them that fear him: and his righteousness upon children's children;
Even upon such as keep his covenant: and think upon his commandments to do them.
The Lord hath prepared his seat in heaven: and his kingdom ruleth over all.
O praise the Lord, ye angels of his, ye that excel in strength: ye that fulfil his commandment, and hearken unto the voice of his words.
O praise the Lord, all ye his hosts: ye servants of his that do his pleasure.

O speak good of the Lord, all ye works of his, in all places of his dominion: praise thou the Lord, O my soul.'

I quote it in full for this reason: as a little child, someone got Tallulah to learn it. Half a century later, in her stage show, she could still quote it in its entirety. If it was that important to Tallulah, it is worth a look. There are worse pieces of wisdom to leave a child. It is full of love, forgiveness and understanding and if Tallulah had a god he was going to have to have a hand long in all three suits!

In all families, there is usually a woman who keeps the family stories, which she hones and polishes to a wholesome familial nugget. The hard edges of fact have been buffed off them, but the hard core of sentiment remains. In my family the ball is passed from Great, Great Aunt Ida, down through Great Aunt Elsie, to Aunt Christine and is now about to be shunted to – well, me – the professional story polisher, if I can be trusted to keep them out of Plays! In the Bankhead family ... Come On Down Auntie Marie Owen! Will's sister, who reports that as Ada lay dying she asked Marie to 'Take care of my baby Eugenia. Tallulah will always be able to take care of herself.'

The witness-preacher wrote, 'She lately came to live here as a bride only twenty-one years of age, she was a beautiful little woman and from the first became devoted to me as her pastor. I was with her during her painful illness and administered Holy Communion. She was perfectly conscious almost to the last and said to me: "Mr Bannister, do you think God will take me to Heaven?" On reporting to her the assurance of our Lord to all who freely turn to him, a sweet smile brightened her beautiful countenance and then, expressing sorrow at leaving her little babe, she seemed to trustfully submit to the will of God.'

Whether her mother got to Heaven or not is not our concern. What we have here is a baby and a two-year old with no mother, and a father who is reeling about in sozzled pieces all over Alabama. Will takes up drinking and is heartbroken. He writes sensitively in his diary:

'Those letters tell the story of our courtship with a tenderer diction than I now can write — for then joy and beautiful anticipations ran from my pen, while now I write in the shadow of the loss while choked with the anguish of absence, the matchless beauty of my bride. I have her wedding gown. She wore it only once. I have never had the courage to look upon its silken folds since she went away to God.'

Will kept his wife's wedding gown. But not his two daughters. They stayed with Grandmother and Grandfather, first in Fayette and then at 'Sunset', the Bankhead family home, in the small mining town of Jasper. Will stayed in Huntsville. He could not and did not contribute towards his children's upkeep. The Grandparents were well off — big, old-money house, two coal-mines, Coca-Cola shares. Will spent what little money he had on drink, women and trouble. He was only twenty-eight and still considered a Big Catch in Huntsville despite probably being alcoholic and sleeping with a loaded gun which he threatened to cock and blow out his brains with as the mood took him.

When he visited his daughters, it was noticeable that he loves, loves, loves Eugenia. Tallulah he ignored, whether this was because she was still just a squib of a baby or because he felt she had killed his wife is not clear. But Grandmother and Grandfather were loving, fierce, and awesome. Tallulah had them both wound round her little Southern finger — something of an achievement seeing as she was fat, unladylike and an illness-magnet, catching measles, mumps, pneumonia, whooping cough, erysipelas (which is, according to *my* Shorter Oxford Dictionary, 'a local febrile disease accompanied by diffused inflammation of the skin; often called "St Anthony's fire" or "the rose".' — poor kid), smallpox and tonsillitis — not a Pears Competition Winner then. Eugenia, meanwhile, developed weak eyes and had to sleep in the daytime and play at night, rather like one of those marsupials you can visit in Midnight World at London Zoo. Tallulah ate everything that wasn't nailed down, then roamed the area, sitting in on the meals of later-eating neighbours. A Dedicated and Zealous Comfort Eater. So the poor grandparents were essentially raising a Bushbaby and a Gannet. The little Bushbaby got to sit next to Daddy when he visited. The Gannet explored the concept of Eating For America. Daddy fondly nicknamed

Eugenia 'Nothing Much'. Tallulah appeared not to have had a nickname, although 'Too Much' pretty much fitted her in every way. In her thrillingly dashing autobiography, (*packed* with Improved-Upon Stories) she tells of coming dangerously close to death at the age of six, when a snake bit her whilst on a picnic with Daddy.

> *'Quick as a flash, Daddy snatched off my panties and sucked the blood from the wound. Subsequently, he was quite ill. He had an abrasion in his gums and the poison infected him.'*

Eugenia tells it like this: Tallulah was never bitten by a snake. Uncle John was bitten by a snake and Will did help out with his treatment. The scar on Tallulah's upper thigh was caused by the lancing of a multi-headed carbuncle.

Now, which one do you believe? Which one do you want to believe?

On her passport application under 'distinguishing marks' Tallulah always wrote 'snakebite'. Whichever story is true, it's all your average Freudian Landmine Site, isn't it?

Grandma Bankhead endeavoured to bring up her granddaughters as Southern Ladies; that is to wear white gloves, Lady-Like (try an exaggerated Southern drawl here) dresses, to mind their manners, be courteous, perform charitable deeds, cultivate the right sort of people and be respectful of one's elders. We shall see in later chapters how well she succeeded in inculcating these qualities in Tallulah. Tallulah was a shouty, gabby, threatening, energetic galoot of a girl – and very good at Tantrums. And as every good Tantrum-thrower knows, it's essential to go purple in the face, hurl yourself to the floor and make an awful lot of LOUD, ALARMING NOISE.

Grandmother Bankhead's ground breaking method of dealing with this was to warn Tallulah she was going to get the bucket, announce she was getting the bucket, announce she was *really* getting the bucket, then *really* get the bucket and then *really* douse the little banshee with a bucketful of cold water.

Guess What? Didn't Work.

Of course, Tallulah felt less loved, less worthy, less everything but less weight than her elder sister. The girls had birthdays a week apart so Daddy elected to celebrate *both* their birthdays on Eugenia's birth date, with a cake between them. How would *you* feel? Yes, dust off that next Tantrum ...

In the kindergarten school play, Eugenia was Rainbow (multi-coloured, radiant and curving). Tallulah got to play Moon (large and round) – although to the end of her life, Eugenia insists that Tallulah was merely one of several raindrops – in fetching brown crêpe paper.

For about ten years, her father was this weepy, unpredictable Big Treat who beerily clasped Eugenia to his chest crying 'Ada, Ada'. Tallulah perfected Showing Off, Cartwheels and Appalling Behaviour to get his attention. With her Grandmother she went once a week to visit the Negro quarter of Jasper, the old lady taking food, a superior's advice and her dirty washing. With her Grandfather, Captain John, she goes electioneering, the perfect occupation for hurling vast amounts of free food (fried chicken, potato salad, anything with mega-calories) down one's gullet and Showing Off – the Chelsea Clinton, John Kennedy Junior, Patty Nixon of 1915. 'I'm Tallulah Bankhead. My Granddaddy's running for Congress. I hope you'll vote for my Granddaddy.'

In 1910, when Captain John and wife make Congress and leave for Washington, Daddy feels once again that he can't look after his little girls, so they are dispatched to Montgomery, to live with his sister, Marie Owen. She was a local columnist, romance writer and, in her later years (get this), a playwright! Her husband is chief historian and archivist for the state of Alabama.

Here are two excerpts from her work from the Montgomery Archives, stored not because her husband was chief archivist, but *surely* for their artistic excellence. Firstly, for the Movie Fans among you, meet the heroine of her (thus far!) unproduced feature film, *Children Of The Night*:

'Lillymay Jenkies, a half-educated school teacher who is secretly a life-insurance agent, enters the scene through the wood's path.'

And even better, from her (thus far!) unpublished novel *Executor with Bond*:

'Jude's heart skipped two beats. They stood looking down at the city for a long, silent moment, hand clasped with hand, shoulder touching shoulder. Then Jude caught her up in his arms and ran with her into the desert.'

Don't you like her? Tallulah certainly did, but mostly because Aunt Marie, domestically, did not run a tight ship and Tallulah did pretty much what she liked, when she liked. Aunt Marie puts the girls into Miss Gussie Woodruff's school, where both did *very well* in Deportment and coasted along in other, less showy, subjects. Tallulah perfects a classy impersonation of the headmistress, who dressed like Judith Anderson as Mrs Danvers in the Fontaine/Olivier film *Rebecca*.

Home to Jasper for the summer holidays. Tallulah's behaviour improving, tantrum-count low, everything going smoothly until bored, impressionable girls have an excellent wheeze: let's get Eugenia to dress up in her dead mother's green taffeta riding costume and impersonate her father's dead love as he comes home from work.

Daddy, who had clearly Had Enough, sends his beloved daughters *as far away as possible* to The East and the Convent of the Sacred Heart, Manhattanville, New York. When The Going Gets Tough, Send In The Nuns! The girls were Episcopalians, so thus not *au fait* with Catholic practices, beliefs, or schools. 'Tallulah' was not a name that impressed the East. Modesty was a big thing in this school and she had to bathe under a nightshirt. Still, it was the only school that would take nine and ten year old girls as boarders. Had to be an institution with high-minded, child-orientated principles.

It must have been absolutely grim and dreadful for the poor little wretches. In the Unbearably Grim School Scenario there are only two ways of going – the Helen Burns of Lowood School path, where you Die Heroically and Stoically in Chapter Three, or The Jane Eyre way – you kick up a fuss and get to appear as the misunderstood heroine for the rest of the book. Tallulah chose the second route.

The Mother Superior called in Will Bankhead, who came and visited them at Christmas and – Mr Fatherly Treats – took his daughters to see *The Whip* at The Manhattan Opera House. The details of the play make me drool with envy – the riot scenes, the full hunt, the train smash, the race-course scene, the chamber of horrors interlude. The rather *warm* nature of the adult intrigues has Tallulah affected in this wise:

> '*By the end of the first act, both of us had wet our pants* [her and Eugenia, that is, *not* Daddy!] *I was a wreck, frantic, red-eyed and dishevelled. I didn't sleep for two nights. I've never recovered!'*

No surprise that this happy family jaunt doesn't make the school any more acceptable to our heroine. Running amok and throwing an inkpot at Mother Superior finally got her sent back to Jasper in disgrace. Where Tallulah went, Eugenia followed and in September 1913 they were sent far away from their loving father, this time to the Mary Baldwin Seminary in Staunton, Virginia. Eugenia managed to get a part in the school play, but Tallulah, turned down because of an untimely acne-visitation – now Spotty as well as Fatty – started as she meant to go on and got drunk on rough cider, turned cartwheels and bit a teacher's hand ...

The girls were invited to leave their second school.

Now, two significant events appear on our heroine's bleak horizon. One, her father, who has been running for election to Congress, suffers a defeat, as a result of a dirty low smear campaign in which his opponents manage to stick him with the nickname 'Little Willy', with the epithet 'drunk', but worse than all this, with being a poor father for 'raising his daughters outside Alabama'! In The South you can ignore them, farm them out, threaten them with your own suicide – but never, *never* send them to school outside Alabama!

Two, she falls in love ... with a nun.

Now at The Convent Of The Visitation, Washington, Eugenia started to moon about young cadets at the Staunton Military Academy, and Tallulah got a Huge Crush on Sister Ignatius. The impeccable Sister Ignatius took Tallulah's side in one of her many school-yard fights and that was it, Cupid's arrow shot rainbows and stars – and Tallulah was in love with her first nun. She did what you do for your first love, hang around to catch a glimpse of them, do little tasks for them that don't need doing, talk about them endlessly and boringly and become, generally speaking, a pain in the kidneys. People with degrees in psychology and such will say she had a crush on this and subsequent nuns because she was motherless and with an absent father. I'd say a) we've hit our first lesbian signifier and b) she had crushes because *Girls do.* This was the 1913 equivalent of being resoundingly in love with Boyzone, The Spice Girls, The Beatles, Leonardo di Caprio, All Saints, Cliff Richard, Princess Diana, any teacher, any sports instructor. In short, anyone unattainable and therefore desirable. For my mother, it was the Scottish soldier on the Crawford Tartan Shortbread Tin. For me, it was Miss Yates, who wore green scarves with navy blue dresses, taught English Literature and always cast herself as the lead in any reading-out-plays-in-class.

Nuns are the perfect love-idol. They wear enveloping black habits so they are mysterious (what's underneath?). They are in love with only God (so no Competition!), and you can't take them out on dates, so you are never going to disappoint them with your non-existent conversation and hopelessly inadequate kissing technique. Also, when you get older and wildly sophisticated, you can incorporate them into dirty jokes.

Tallulah had a long line of nun-crushes. And, later, a cloister full of nun-stories.

Another great milestone and good Fairy Story standby. In 1914, Will provided his daughters with a Wicked Stepmother. Against family wishes and without mentioning it to his daughters, he married Florence McGuire, a twenty-five year old daughter of a lawyer friend who had been his secretary, and therefore wasn't *quite* the right class. She wasn't wicked, she didn't behave like a mother and she did the new girlfriend thing of getting along with the boyfriend's children.

Suddenly, Tallulah becomes very fond of her father. Call me suspicious, call me mean-spirited, but could this have *anything* to do with his having bought his first car, a spiffy Hudson with ising-glass windows ('you can roll them right down, in case there's a change in the weather'), and *en famille* drives-out into the country? A trip to Myrtle Beach, South Carolina, sees that other Big News event in a girl's early life – the arrival of her first period, which Tallulah welcomes by trumpeting 'Stop the car, Daddy, I'm dying', from the back seat. The fondness for Daddy and the peace continues until Daddy decides, ever the clever psychologist, to send Eugenia to The Margaret Booth School for Young Ladies, Montgomery, and Tallulah to the Dunbar Holy Cross Academy, Washington. Tallulah, separated from her sister for the first time goes even more ape-shit than usual.

She found local, scholarly fame as the worst, most delinquent pupil ever to attend The Dunbar Holy Cross Academy, Washington.

She bunked off school one evening to see Alla Nazimova in *War Brides* at the Princess Theater. Here's how notorious lesbian lover Mercedes Acosta describes Nazimova:

> *'She represented Imperial Russia in a thrilling tableau, dressed as a cossack and waving the czarist flag. She had thick black hair which stood out from her head and her eyes were the only truly purple-coloured eyes I have ever seen.'*

Nazimova was stunning, camp, emotional, exotic, lesbian, and numbered among her lovers were Mercedes Dacosta, Dolly Wilde (niece of Oscar, For Heaven's sake!) and Natasha Rambovas. She had a place she called The Garden Of Allah with a *moon parlour* and a swimming pool in the shape of the Crimean sea (we *all* expire of Envy!). Nazimova hit poor Sister Ignatius right out of the stadium as crush material.

Tallulah took to drooping her eyes and fainting all over the place in imitation of Nazimova. In a fat, spotty, naughty girl this must have been something. Fortunately, some guardian angel of the Holy Cross was on watch that day – and here was the pay-off for having Faith – the beleagured holy school's prayers are answered and Tallulah Nazimova was moved schools to be with Eugenia once again.

In 1916, Will finally made it to Congress, so his daughters were enrolled at the swanky Fairmount Seminary in Washington. Tallulah studied classical music, a little piano playing, violin playing – and now it's Ugly Duckling to Swan time – she grew her hair long and lovely, lost twenty pounds in weight, her spots left for some other poor kid's face and she started doing her lips à la Nazimova, with bright red lipstick. And Whack, she turned into a Swan! Her luck was in, she fell ill with a virus, which knocked off some more weight, got her out of Fairmount and off to Atlantic City for a sea air cure with a fetching full-length sealskin coat to keep out the chill.

Aunt Louise took her, so they stayed in the best hotel, where, as luck had it, Nora Bayes, 'The Greatest Single Woman Singing Comedienne In The World', who was appearing for vast sums in Vaudeville, was also staying. Tallulah insisted on seeing Bayes perform seven times (now that's a Big Crush). she staked out the foyer, got to meet Bayes and got her autograph.

Tallulah is now fourteen, pushy and gorgeous, starstruck and dramastruck. Her homelife has been bizarre and tragic, her family life dysfunctional and competitive.

What future is there for a histrionic, bad-tempered, tantrum-throwing, exhibitionist, sex-mad, girl?

Why, what future but that of an actress?

What world but entertainment?

Unstable trinitrotoluene

Scene: FROM OFFSTAGE WE HEAR A TEENAGE
                        GIRL SHOUTING THROUGH TWO STOREYS
                        AT HER MOTHER ...

Sarah: *I'm not a Young Madam! ...*

Picture the fifteen year old girls in your own life. Remember, if you are a woman, what you were like at that age. You were Unstable T.N.T. If you are a man, recall the terror we conjured up in you, you spotty little oik. Yes, Naked Terror.

Teenage girls are the species who can reduce grown parents to tears, induce experienced teachers to take months off for stress-related illnesses, bus-conductors to hurl themselves off buses and political parties to consider incarceration, institutionalised beating and Kinder, Kuchen und Kirken as politically-viable containment options. They are good at shop-lifting, lying, blackmail, intrigue, intimidation, threats, manipulation, belligerent arm-folding and flirtatious come-ons. They are bad at compromise, truth, rigour, humility, self-knowledge, abstinence and the word *love*.

There is a myth floating about that teenagers are insecure. It's not true. At fifteen, boy, you don't *think* you know everything, you *know* you know everything. You are never going to be so certain, so smart, so cool, so *where it's at,* ever, ever, ever again. Maturity is knowing you know nothing. Fifteen is Certainty.

Our heroine is now fifteen. She's completed her formal education. She's

Who is She?

The young lady whose photograph is printed above has been chosen by the judges as a winner in our Screen Opportunity Contest. But who is she? We do not know. Her letter, containing her application blank, with her name and her address, was lost among fifty thousand other letters and packages, and her identity remains a mystery. But the judges, resolved to retain the utmost fairness in their decisions, did not put another in her place among the winners. Will the lady of mystery, who is having the door to success in filmdom held open until she arrives, kindly communicate with the editor of PICTURE-PLAY MAGAZINE immediately upon seeing this?

'... A SORT OF CINDERELLA PROBLEM REVERSED ...'

excelled in deportment. She's majored in Delinquency, Intimidation and Tantrum. Does she, like the nice girl in *What Katy Did*, fall off a swing and learn patience and kindness? Does she, like Jo in *Little Women*, cut off her hair and get tamed by a cuddly German professor? Does she, like Jane Eyre, end up with a 'dear Reader, I married Him. End of Story'?

No. She gets a break.

PICTURE-PLAY MAGAZINE JUNE 1917
SCREEN OPPORTUNITY CONTEST

Your last chance to enter.
Marjorie Rambeau now a judge.

The end of Picture-Play's screen opportunity contest, and the bright beginning of twelve motion-picture careers, which will automatically follow, are both close at hand. The last chance you will have to make your future one of these twelve has arrived. If you have not already become a contestant, now is the time.

No doubt you know just what the result of this contest means to the winners. Twelve people, regardless of age and sex, are to be chosen from entries by the judges, and these twelve people will have their expenses paid to New York and be paid a salary of at least twenty-five dollars a week while they act in a feature picture. Each of the winners will be given a real part, not that of an extra, in a five-reel production made by Frank Powell Producing Corporation, and personally directed by Frank Powell, the man who discovered Theda Bara and Blanche Sweet.

Now, while us mature, suspicious, enquiring, wimpy grown-ups might fill our heads with awkward, awful doubt such as 'Cheap Publicity Stunt?', 'Dodgy Deal?', 'What Part?' and 'Who the Hell Is Blanche Sweet?', Confident Fifteen just thinks … 'I'll win that!' and enters.

Tallulah sends off a photograph – best profile (sexier than full-face), large fur collar (promotes opulence and softens the jawline) and wide-brimmed hat (promotes sophistication, draws attention to eyes). And sits back, confidently waiting to win.

Pages of the calendar flip by – June, July, – it might as well rain ... until September:

ANNOUNCEMENT OF CONTEST WINNERS

Judges' complete decision of
Screen Opportunity Winners.

At last the anxiously awaited announcement of contest winners can be made. On the first twelve pages of this issue of PICTURE-PLAY MAGAZINE the photographs of the winners appear.

These pages, as readers of this magazine know, are reserved for the photographs of screen stars and in devoting this space to our winners we wish to imply the hope that they will some day be shining luminaries in the film firmament.'

The degree of brightness with which shining luminaries Henrietta L. Grant, Lela Sue Campbell, and Myrtle Owen Anderson, (mother of two, Tulsa, Oklahoma) sparkled in the film firmament is not my concern here, Gentle Reader.

The last picture in the twelve pages normally reserved for photographs of screen stars, has the caption:

WHO IS SHE?

It is interesting to note that after the winners were selected it was found that one fair beauty among them was unidentified. It was discovered that her name and address did not appear on the photograph and – pity of pities – her letter and application blank had been lost. At first the predicament seemed hopeless. In fairness to the winner the judges did not wish to be forced to substitute someone in her place. It seemed to them that it was a sort of Cinderella problem reversed. Her name, which corresponded to the slipper, was missing and had to be found.

The search for it was still going on. It was decided to publish her picture along with all the other winners in the hope that she would see it and then come forward and make herself known'.

So certain are you, at fifteen, that you will win, you forget to fill out the application form.

So keen is practically every young thing to get into movies, that many meretricious young ladies had themselves photographed in flattering furs and wide-brimmed hats. Fortunately our heroine had on her side, not necessarily in order of influence, a duplicate photo and a letter, on headed, State-embossed paper, from a Grandfather in The Senate.

The glass slipper fitted. Tallulah Brockman Bankhead was indeed the official Cinderella. Now all Cinders has to do is convince The Family.

With Daddy in Congress, and Granddaddy in The Senate, the entire Brockman Bankhead Dynasty were living in apartments at 1868 Columbia Road, Washington; parents on the sixth floor, grandparents on the seventh. Tallulah, tellingly, was living on the seventh floor. Florence was over the first rush of 'let's all get along'. Grandparents were hopeful that Will would finally spend time with his children. Now Tallulah had a chance to go to New York.

The Family debates the notion.

Grandmother Bankhead, sensible woman, is against the idea. Florence, her stepmother, spookily is all in favour of Tallulah going. Daddy Will can't make his mind up. A defenceless, motherless girl in New York? Who will pay for her? Finally, the Senator Grandaddy swings it. It is the opportunity of a lifetime, he will foot the bills, and his daughter, Tallulah's Aunt Louise, who is mourning the death of her eighteen year old son, William, and is widowed from her first husband and just separated from her second, will be her chaperone. Aunt Louise can get over her son's death, keep an eye on her niece and, as she is currently living with Olga Davis (William's fiancée and a singer who also wants to be a Big Star), Tallulah can stay with her too!

Thus The Family will have full control over her. What Could Go Wrong?

Well, Here Goes ...

Eugenia, Will's other carefully-nurtured, impeccably-raised daughter, runs off and marries Morton Hoyt, the son of the deceased Solicitor-General of the United States. He's the right class of society, but he's just one in a long line of crushes, so we are all of us certain *it can't last*. In an 'It Happened One Night' scenario, Will tracks his daughter down and snatches her before the union is consummated. Eugenia was later to prove her reliability by marrying Morton two more times.

This debacle naturally detracted everyone's attention from The New York end of things, where things were going a little pear-shaped. The promoter contracted by Picture-Play to launch the twelve shining luminaries into the film firmament had proved unreliable. Neither he nor the funds were in evidence. While Henrietta L. Gant, Lela Sue Campbell and Myrtle Owen Anderson might have given up and gone home, Tallulah's family had influence. Strings were pulled, favours called in and Knox Julian, Grandaddy's Man In New York got the project up and running again. Tallulah and her fellow pinpoints of light in Picture-Play's newly-discovered galaxy worked for three weeks, for $75 in total, on *The Wishful Girl*, directed by Del Henderson and John O'Brien. It starred a Picture-Play winner, Françoise du Barry. Sadly, no complete print exists of this forgotten masterpiece.

Aunt Louise, suffering horribly no doubt from grief, spent a lot of time with spiritualists, trying to contact her dead son. One did indeed report a psychic call from William, who offered his grieving Mother the information 'Morning, Mother, it's always morning'. The rest just took her money. She tried, in her way, to help both hopeful stars in her care along their career trajectories. Tallulah, with letters of introduction from Knox Julian visits Benjamin Hampton (who, as vice-president of the America Tobacco Company, had large shares in Goldwyn and Rex Beach Pictures) Edward Seldon, a play broker, John Rhinock, a theatrical impresario and David Belasco of Famous Players. Nothing came of the visits directly. Tallulah decided that Aunt Louise was probably to blame for her stasis. She turns sixteen on 31 January and on 23 February receives a letter from her father:

> 'I intended to send you a telegram, but it slipped my memory. May sweet sixteen be the threshold of your final dreams. I have no son, and maybe never will have. I will depend on you to represent your father and your grandfather by making a real and lasting career as an artist in your chosen profession. It is a fine thing to contemplate how powerful a factor the screen has become on the thought and conduct of the world, and how great the possibilities it offers to you – my daughter. But don't forget, when you get your real chance, don't forget that it takes steady sacrifice and inconvenience. There is no royal road to the top anywhere. Let us know your prospects, and keep me advised where and in what picture I may "look upon thine image."'

Ah, the Bankhead Parents. Fantastic on the wise words, hopeless at the hands-on.

In February also, Aunt Louise and The Young Hopefuls moved into the Algonquin Hotel. We *all* know the reputation of The Algonquin – apart from Aunt Louise, who chose it because *she* knew that Commander Evangeline Booth, Il Duce of The Salvation Army, stayed there when she was in town saving the souls of New York.

The 'I'm Here' visits finally paid off. Lee and Jake, the Shubert Brothers, asked to see her. They put on plays. They made Al Jolson famous. They were smart enough to know that Big Broadway Hits start off out of town. And they offered Tallulah a walk-on in their new show *The Squab Farm*, starring Alma Tell and Gladys Sinclair. It opened at The Bijou Theater on 45th Street in March 1918. Knox Julian played a publicity blinder with a full column in the Plays and Players Section of the New York Evening Telegram with a 'beautiful young unknown from important political family' angle. Alma Tell – the star – got two lines. The play got stinking reviews: 'a garish travesty of life in the movies, all in bad taste'. The lucky walk-ons get a mention: 'There are four young girls who might be better in the care of their mothers'. The play closed three weeks later – one can imagine the atmosphere in the dressing

LIONEL, ETHEL AND JOHN BARRYMORE, TALLULAH COULD NEVER DECIDE WHO
SHE WAS MORE IN LOVE WITH; ETHEL OR JOHN

rooms and trusts that the most publicity-rich young walk-on, when around
Alma Tell, stayed quiet, laid low and kept her back to the wall at all times.

Tallulah contained her disappointment over *The Squab Farm*'s early death,
because Granddaddy's acquaintance, Ivan Abramson, a Russian independent
film producer, cast her in *When Men Betray*. She got her first good review:

> ' ... exquisite of feature, dainty of form, deliciously feminine, and with a pair of
> large eyes that have the power of expressing all their emotions in a glance.
> Her appearance brings with it the feeling that with her the very atmosphere
> is surcharged with energy.'

Close readers will spot that this is a review of her *sexiness*. The reviewer fancies the socks off her. Her *acting* is without mention. The film sinks without trace.

However, she was still at The Algonquin, and The Algonquin was overrun with Loose Tickets dealing in sexiness, wit, intelligence, affairs, smart-talking and *Names*. Tallulah was in Teenage Aspirant Heaven. On the one hand Commander Evangeline Booth *did* stay there, on the other, the whole joint was full of lesbians, gays, bisexuals and sexual experimenters. There was Dorothy Parker, musical comedy star Elsie Janis, Frank Crowninshield (publisher of *Vanity Fair*), Douglas Fairbanks Junior, Constance Collier, Ina Claire, Anita Loos, Laurette Taylor, Rex Beach and three Barrymores – Ethel, John and Lionel. Oh, and six-foot tall, blonde, bisexual Jobyna Howland, model for the first Gibson Girl. This was not a society for the tight nuclear family. Tallulah, in later years, could never decide who she was more in love with around then, John or Ethel Barrymore.

She was making good career connections. Top Networking. And from sixteen onwards, such a solid grounding in sexual live-and-let-live-ery. She met Estelle Winwood who would become her friend for life. Estelle was an English actress, sixteen years her senior and appearing in the hugely successful, first-ever Pulitzer-Prized *Why Marry Me?* on Broadway. Jobyna Howland had a mouth as dirty and gritty as the sandtray of a cockatiel's cage. When she said to Tallulah 'Take that cigarette out of your mouth, you infant', Tallulah did. Spot the Role Model here. Tallulah was still mouthy, pushy and rushy. She was emotional, a tears-bucket and needy. She was generous with her crushes. She was beautiful and young. Her father was a Congressman, her Grandfather a Senator. The Algonquin Set couldn't fail to love her.

1918 turned into 1919. Olga got discouraged with not being discovered and returned to Montgomery. The relationship between Tallulah and her long-suffering, spirit-seeking Aunt-Chaperone became strained on account of incompatibility, teenage truth-management and – finally –Tallulah spending an afternoon alone with a young male photographer, during which Something Went On, and semi-nude pictures were taken. Tallulah remained, technically at least, a virgin, and always swore her first lover had been a woman (But who? – the big problem with decades of Homosexual Repression is that a biographer does *not* get to find out!). Aunt and Niece had a row where Tallulah told her in graphic – if inaccurate – detail what had gone on. But Aunt Louise had had enough. 'I do not believe there is a human being alive who can control her' she wrote to Senator Bankhead. Aunt Louise enlisted in The Red Cross and went to nurse the poorly in France.

Well, another aunt has to be put on Tallulah Watch, so Aunt Marie is hauled in. Even her *laissez-faire* way of chaperonage is strained to its limits. She is appalled by Tallulah's newly-acquired skill with foul language and very perturbed by the amount of attention she is receiving from the six foot bisexual Jobyna. But Tallulah, now the teenage *Eloise* of The Algonquin, was impossible to handle, so Aunt Marie goes back home to Montgomery.

A story: Tallulah, lying in bed one night, hears someone pounding on her door. She opens it to a desperate actress, who says 'Have you got a douche bag? I've just been raped!' Tallulah says 'No, but I have an enema bag. Will that do?'

Again, it feels like a good story that has been polished up and improved upon over the years but the essence of it remains. This is a teenage girl living in the anonymity of a large hotel. Tallulah is probably petted, played with and set up to amuse. Yet again she is in an environment with No Boundaries.

Granddaddy tries to educate, nurture and raise from afar. Delegation. Tallulah is instructed to take Sunday dinner with (*Very* Family Values) The Cauble Family and telephone them regularly. They were true and trusted friends of The Senator's who lived in New York. Tallulah was to be Family with a Family she had never met. Knox Julian was to continue to check on her character and career. He hit upon the clever ploy of asking Frank Case, the manager of The Algonquin, to keep an eye on her. The manager was reported as saying 'I can either run a busy hotel or I can look after Tallulah Bankhead. I can't do both!'

So, Nobody is looking after Tallulah.

A glove salesman, now working in movies, Samuel Goldfish, took a shine to Tallulah and cast her in her second silent film *Thirty A Week*, opposite the gorgeous Tom Moore. Like *When Men Betray,* it was no *Battleship Potemkin*. Samuel Goldfish changed his name to Goldwyn and went on to Rule The World.

Granddaddy was sending her fifty dollars a week. Half of this went on her room. The other twenty-five did for every other living expense. When her One Good Outfit was being cleaned, she simply stayed in her room, the state of which was such a standing joke with the other Algonquinites, that they considered having a whip-round to buy her another. Joked, Considered and Discussed. But Didn't.

She wasn't getting any work at all. Grandaddy, Daddy, Knox Julian all believed that films were where her future lay. But the two silent disasters she had worked in had given her a huge antipathy towards film. She wanted to go on The Stage.

She ran around schmoozing, networking and telling creative lies to Granddaddy about the number of offers, chances and possibilities she had in the pipeline but by halfway through 1919 she hadn't had any theatre work for more than a year. Edward Seldon wrote to The Senator 'Don't let Tallulah stay here too long if she does not get an engagement. We don't want her to get shopworn. New York is no place for an idle girl to be.'

Without a regular chaperone to give the impression of respectability and, more importantly, show that The Family is doing its duty, Tallulah is in danger of being called home. Senator and Congressman Bankhead are beginning to agree that their little girl is not at her safest in strange and dangerous New York and they are just a little concerned that Tallulah might be getting a taste for hard liquor – just like Daddy.

Luckily, Aunt Louise, with the Great War now over, returned from her brief nursing career in France and pitched up at The Algonquin. Tallulah was delighted to see her because, a) she adored her Aunt Louise, b) she had a chaperone again and, c) she was starving so Aunt Louise took her out for an enormous meal. Aunt Louise resumed her role as German Shepherd Dog, writing with rare perspicacity to The Senator 'I think she would rather starve and go naked than give up the theatre.' She was obviously unaware that starving and going naked *are* the theatre.

Mrs. Cauble, the Erzatz Family Mother, recalls 'During one visit, Tallulah complained of a headache. She asked to lie down and went into a bedroom. There issued from the room a cry, almost a howl, which frightened all of us. Tallulah, drawn and frantic, came out of the room and said to me "I've got to go on the stage." I never saw one her age so nervous.'

In early summer, 1919, Tallulah was offered a job in Summer Stock. In Somerville, Massachusetts. Summer Stock was like weekly rep – you rehearsed next week's play all day, then performed this week's play in the evening, then you had to go have a drink in the bar, because you were so high after the performance so you stayed up till the early hours, then up at eight the next morning drinking a lot of water and coffee ready to start rehearsing at nine o'clock. Tallulah stayed the two weeks she was offered. She discovered that she learnt lines very easily. The company manager asked her to stay on, and go with them to Baltimore, but as she told Granddaddy 'I can't possibly do it, Granddaddy honey, because I would be dead'.

And she's back to the darkened room, the headaches and the revolving-door of gloom of an actor out of work ...

The winter before, in Washington – visiting for her sister's coming-out party – a young fling, Robert Carrere, had taken her to the town's most popular play, Rachel Crother's *39 East*, starring Constance Binney and Henry Hull. Like all very new young actresses with no experience, Tallulah felt that Binney had really not got to the guts of the part – she, Tallulah could obviously do it much, much better, and it would be a kind, brave and honest act to tell Miss Binney all this. Fortunately, guardian angels must have stepped in and stopped this Gun Fight At The OK Corral Scenario. The play was produced by Mary Kirkpatrick, a Southern Gal and friend of Senator Bankhead. Some of

Tallulah's views on her performance did get back to the star.

The play had come to town in April, got nice notices, and was doing good business. It was the sentimental story of the eponymous New York boarding house and its inhabitants, who were all 'appealing, entertaining and typically feminine'. Tallulah heard on The Algonquin Grapevine that Rachel Crothers, whose work was 'always produced entirely under her own supervision' [my Heroine!] was looking for an understudy for Miss Binney, who liked to take long weekends during the summer. The understudy would then travel with the second company on tour.

Tallulah, her Granddaddy's granddaughter, went the Southern Old Pals route and hunted down Mary Kirkpatrick on the street. Miss Kirkpatrick thought Tallulah's chances were small. Miss Crothers was unlikely to hire someone with so little experience, 'even if she were the President's daughter'. Well, she was the *Senator's* daughter, so, she got an audition at the Broadhurst Theater.

Tallulah read, impressed and got herself hired. She got $100 a week, a part-time maid and a clothing allowance. Sidney Blackmer was hired to understudy Henry Hull. Blackmer and Tallulah Did Not Get On.

In *39 East* the female lead role is Penelope Penn, a small-town minister's daughter who has come to The Big City to look for choir work, not for herself, but to put her brother through college (Loveable or what?). She stays at the lodging house of the title, looks for the perfect choir, falls in with a Low Dog who spirits her off to Central Park to have his way with her, only to be saved from Sin and Degradation by the timely intervention of the Henry Hull/Sidney Blackmer juve lead.

Rachel Crothers who clearly developed a Big Crush on Tallulah, suggested she study diction, French and ballet. They hung out together at the Coffee House Club on West 45th Street. A lot of the rehearsals took place at the playwright's apartment and sometimes, Tallulah stayed over.

She spent a lot of time watching Miss Binney from the wings. When she and

Blackmer finally went on together for the first time, Daddy, The Stepmother and Eugenia came up to see the performance. Grandmother Tallulah sents a note saying 'I know you will make my name more famous than ever.'

Remember, she is only sixteen, she has had no training whatsoever, and she's centre stage for the first time. How she copes is by simply copying, gesture for gesture, intonation for intonation, move for move, the actress she is understudying.

The key scene, in Central Park, requires her to take off her sunbonnet, leave it on a bench and exit, leaving the hat as a big clue for Sydney Blackmer to spot and deduce that our heroine is in trouble, and thus let The Plot and the ensuing scenes kick in.

Now, what happens if you go on stage unprepared, improperly rehearsed and with very little directorial help is this − it becomes *very* hard to remember how to do difficult tasks like walking and speaking at the same time; everyday objects such as sunbonnets take on a poltergeist-like life of their own and hurl themselves about everywhere. And you fail to learn that you are supposed to *help* other people on stage to perform *their* job.

The sunbonnet got put down wherever Tallulah ended up. In places where Blackmer's character could not remotely come across it, in places on stage where Blackmer the actor could not spot it without losing his character and moves. The show reports will mention it landing in the upstage lake, the downstage right rocks and even, one night, on the head of the working swan.

Blackmer was beside himself with fury [and I'm on his side]. He begged Tallulah, in that recognisable actor's voice of controlled venom to 'put the hat on the bench. Just put it on the bench.' Tallulah, adopting the *Intuitive* Actress Defence, explained to him that she had too much emoting to do to be consistent about the hat.

Backstage Atmosphere steams. Tallulah retaliates by standing in the revealing beam of the upstage lights while waiting in the wings. The thus transparency of her dress, and the rude back-chat with them, has all the backstage crew on her side. 'If you've got it, flaunt it' was her early motto.

Already − onstage and offstage − she is impersonating women older, wiser, and more experienced than herself.

It is all going to get tricky ...

HITCHCOCK'S 'LIFEBOAT': TALLULAH WORE NO UNDERWEAR FOR THE
ENTIRE FIFTEEN WEEK SHOOT

The four horsewomen of the Algonquin

It is 1919. She is sixteen. And for the next three years, Tallulah is a teenage girl actor in New York.

The Great War has ended. Millions of young men lie dead or wounded or shellshocked from those twin glorious twentieth century inventions – trench warfare and mustard gas. The Chinese Communist Party is founded. The Irish Civil War breaks out. Charlie Chaplin makes the wonderful silent film *The Kid*. Pirandello writes *Six Characters In Search Of An Author*. Faisal is king of Iraq; Fuad is king of Egypt. There will be a Washington Conference on Disarmament. Women doing men's work during the war will, as usual, now be encouraged to go back to being wives and mothers and give back men's jobs to men. In fashion, as in society, there is an untrammelling. Stays are put off. Corsets are out.

After Great Victories, beyond Awful Defeats, people want to party. In New York, young people who hang around with, work in and know theatre, have a new title – Kid flappers. Flappers lived to burn out through partying, sex, drink and drugs. Kid flappers just do it younger. It is this particular age's term for teenager, adolescent, young soul rebel, teddy boy, Bow Street Dandy, hippy, crusty – choose one. They show their maturity and *savoir-faire* in the time-honoured way – taking drugs, smoking everything poisonous you can roll into a tube and stick in your mouth, drinking strong spirits (here – bourbon), fucking everybody, accepting anything free (jewellery, flowers, gifts, meals, drinks, drugs, sexually-transmitted diseases), despising anyone who doesn't speak your language of 'crazy, divine, shit, darling, mad'. A god isn't 'divine'; a person is. A rabid dog isn't 'crazy'; a dance is. 'Quite' isn't a qualifying term; it's an absolute ('Quite the best dancer', 'Quite the sweetest man'). 'Simply' means 'completely', as in 'Simply everybody loves her'.

In this heady semantic soup, Tallulah started working on her keynote vocabulary and delivery. She's going to spend the rest of her life in Olympic Standard Word Tennis Tournaments. She'll need good trainers, constant practice, and top seed match experience. She'll get it. 'Divine', 'Darling' and 'Shit' will be the Holy Trinity of her distinctive vocabulary; her delivery will be a phrase or group of phrases with a single stress, as in;

'But Ethel Darling, you *are* too fat'

or

'If you've got it darling, why not *flaunt* it?'

and

'nobody can be exactly like me. Even *I* have trouble doing it.'

[For those of you reading out loud, here's a Tallulah Bankhead Master Class. Try this. Copy Bette Davis in *Whatever Happened To Baby Jane*. The line 'But Grace, you *are* in a wheelchair' – Well done!]

She's a good mimic. She has a very good ear for dialects and speech patterns. She has a wide range in her speaking voice. She can sort of sing in tune. She comes from a Southern family who can talk to competition standard. The people at The Algonquin encourage their Girl Pet to chat on. She starts to become a character who might say something amusing, outrageous, glib, memorable ...

Between 1918 and 1922, she appeared in nine plays, all in New York Theaters. *The Squab Farm* had 45 performances; in *39 East*, Tallulah got to go on 6 times, *Footloose* got 32 performances; *Nice People* got 120; *Everyday* at The Bijou Theater played for 30 nights; *Danger* at the 39th Street got 79 performances and *No, Sirree!*, a one-off performance. *Her Temporary Husband* ran for 92 performances and *The Exciters* at the Times Square Theater ran for 43 performances. For 448 evenings of 1,825 days Tallulah was working. The rest of the time, she was up for kid flappery.

Tallulah encountered her first political activism when the cast of *39 East* and six other stage productions went on strike to demand improved working conditions and more equitable contracts. Membership of American Actors Equity wasn't mandatory, but Tallulah, on Granddaddy's advice, had become a member. Knox Julian was against her involving herself in a strike. Tallulah was all for it. Actors love a strike. You get to play politically-conscious, serious-thinking, courageous fighters for justice and seekers of wisdom and truth in a real scenario. You can pretend to be doing a real job. You are de Niro in *Raging Bull*. You are Marlon Brando in *On The Waterfront*. You are Sally Field in almost anything.

Actors Equity organised a rally at The Old Lennox Opera House. Tallulah invites Ethel, Lionel and John Barrymore along (Old Equity Ploy – get *names* involved!), and plays the usherette who showed the sympathetic audience to their seats, taking their entrance fee which, in direct action, is *always* 'Give as much as you can'. The target set for the rally is $100,000.

Tallulah, burning with revolutionary zeal, took the stage to pledge $100 of Granddaddy's money – hey, if a US Senator could give money – .everybody could! They couldn't. The rally raised less than $50,000. Granddaddy responded to his granddaughter's new-found politicisation by stumping up for the donation – and buying her her first evening dress. The Rosa Luxembourg *de ces jours*. Not.

Her letters to Granddaddy at the time showed she would not be any sort of Vanessa Redgrave – committed political actress.

'I joined Actors Equity because it was the right thing to do. All the very biggest stars in the profession belong and it's a wonderful organisation. The Barrymores all belong and if you don't you are called a scab and are blacklisted and they called *39 East* to strike so of course I did. I couldn't play alone anyway and besides it was the right thing to do.'

So there. Got that, committed union activists everywhere?

Sometimes we get ill. It is our body's way of saying 'Enough. Don't hurl any more Hard Liquor, Impossible To Digest Food So Late At Night, and Stressful Partying down your gullet.' Tallulah is attacked by awful, rebounding stomach pains at the Algonquin – publicly, in the lobby of course – and is rushed to St Elizabeth's Hospital with a burst appendix. These days it is an unpleasant, but relatively safe experience – they cut you up, whip it out, sew up the neat little wound, feed you antibiotics and try to get you up and out of bed as quickly as possible. You are known as 'relatively minor surgery'. But this is 1919. Pre-antibiotics. Dangerous operation. You lie around, packed in ice and hope nothing goes poisonous. Tallulah is unlucky. She's gangrenous so she gets peritonitis and is very, very close to dying. She's kept in hospital for six weeks. When she comes out, the Actors Strike is over and she's sent home to recuperate.

Washington is now home. Sister Eugenia, so carefully saved by the intervention of her family from marriage to the dashing Morton Hoyt some years earlier, is now formally engaged, with parental approval ... to Morton Hoyt. He is a drunk, but is son to the late Solicitor General of the entire United States and both his sisters are published novelists. He's connected. Eugenia boasts to Tallulah about her love life, Tallulah boasts to Eugenia about hers. Tallulah has signed a contract to go on the road for nine months with *39 East*. She gets a doctor's certificate detailing her frail state of health, gets out of the contract and returns to the quiet, restorative atmosphere of the Algonquin Hotel.

And Tallulah sets about, deliberately or not, becoming memorable.

The Playwright Zoe Akins turned her into a character, Eva Lovelace, in her play, later filmed as *Morning Glory*. Played by Katherine Hepburn in the flim version, Eva Lovelace was the cleaned-up, arty version of Tallulah – an ingénue in love with 'Theatre' and 'Art'. She chattered, starved for her talent, and, at parties, performed the balcony scene from *Romeo and Juliet* – so artistic, cultured and serious was she. The real Tallulah didn't do Shakespeare at parties, she did impersonations and showing off. Her favourite impersonation was Ethel Barrymore, which she performed at her first Condé

Nast party, in front of Ethel Barrymore. The porky Miss Barrymore said 'But your impersonation makes me look so fat.' Adorable, speak-your-mind Tallulah replied 'But Ethel darling, you *are* fat.' Ethel whacked her one across the face [I'm with Ethel]. It is to both their credits that they remained friends.

Alexander Woollcott, wit and drama critic, universally known as Louisa May Woollcott, who, for a theatre visit wore pebble-thick glasses (not his fault) and a scarlet-lined opera cape (his fault) and who, according to Anita Loos, once confided in her weepily that he would 'never be a mother' took Tallulah to see the cult Maeterlinck hit *Aglaveine and Selysette*. It was one of those Emperor's New Clothes kind of shows where everybody was being impressed and enchanted until someone was brave enough to blow the whistle on it and everybody could then admit that they didn't understand it at all and breathe a collective sigh of philistine relief. Tallulah, meaning to say sagely 'There's more to this than meets the eye', came out with 'There's less to this than meets the eye', a mistake but cleverer, more original and a lot more on the nose than she meant. Louisa May quotes it about. O. O. McIntyre, a dim bulb and Round Table Algonquin Wannabe, wrote up the remark with 'Tallulah Bankhead is beginning to rival Dorothy Parker's reputation as a wit.' It didn't get him onto the Round Table and it didn't get him the lifelong affection of Ms Parker ... But it got Tallulah noticed again.

Tallulah is like the Lorelei Lee character in Anita Loos' *Gentlemen Prefer Blondes*: ' ... like a radio. You listen to it all day long, squawking out rubbish. And just when you cain't stand it no longer and you gonna throw it through the winder ... it comes out with something good.'

She wrote to Grandmother 'Precious Mamma, they all think your little namesake is very clever.' They *all* didn't. They thought she was a joke, but they liked her. They had no great opinion of her acting. She was their Teenage Tigger.

Rachel Crothers gave Tallulah a lot of her work during these years (that's the way to do it, chaps, get a playwright in love with you). In 1921 she cast Tallulah as Hallie Livingston in *Nice People*. Katherine Cornell was Eileen

Baxter Jones. Francine Larrimore was Theodorea. This play seems to have been one of those shows that capture a moment, a way of being, like *Shopping and Fucking* or *Mojo* today, or like *Look Back In Anger* in the fifties. The young characters were kid flappers who were modelled on the set Tallulah hung out with, or the kid flappers modelled themselves on the characters created from them – there was always a murkiness on which way the influence goes. An old, smart character gave us an editorial overview of the kid flappers, of 'the emptiness, the soullessness of it all. I've been here three days and I haven't heard her nor any of her friends say a single word or express a thought about anything on earth but their clothes and their motors and themselves. If they were common little upstarts and parvenus it would be easy to understand. But *nice people!'*

Okay, it's not Becket. But Tallulah is clearly in *the state of the art piece about the people the establishment is scared of.*

They said things like ...

> Hallie: *I adore a man who is absolutely mad about me and yet who controls himself in that perfectly marvellous way.*

or

> Eileen: *Well, I must say I like sort of a frank flash of pash once in a while – so you know where you're at.*

and

> Theodorea: *Oh, I don't know. I'm not so keen about so much self-control.*

Francine Larrimore butched up on stage and *wore overalls!* The play explored the overarcing moral code of the day daringly. The heroine spends the night with a male friend – shock, horror outrage – but a plot character appears to prove that ... *nothing happened.* The cast was mostly gay but only the overalls appeared on stage. Tallulah played herself, the kid flapper, smoking and drinking *real* bourbon. She got the 'someone to watch' notices whereas the Butch Overall part got the sensation mention. A twenty-one year old Noel Coward went to see it. He hated the play and loved the cast – learning his 'first lesson in American acting, which was the technique of realising first, which lines in the script are superfluous and second, knowing when and how to throw them away.'

Tallulah, during this period, went around looking like a true teenager, wearing her 'one good dress' until it could almost stand up and attend parties on its own. She kept her hair in impeccable condition by washing it only in *Energine dry-cleaning fluid*! She cut a dash, but what with the chain-smoking and her hair-regime, it's lucky she didn't set herself *and* the town on fire!

She behaved with true teenage money-wizardry. She and Estelle Winwood decided it would be a smart move to employ a French maid to teach them French. They would thus gain impressive international sophistication and be the envy of all their acquaintances. Tallulah, on $50 a week, employed the French maid at $25 a week. But the French girl was here to learn English, so insisted on speaking only English and Tallulah was too cowed to sack her. French fluency was not achieved.

She swanned around with no money in her purse. With only four cents to her name, she had to borrow one penny to pay the streetcar fare to reach a movie-casting audition with John Barrymore. When asked how she thought she was going to get back, it was clear – Thought had nothing to do with it.

She and three girl Kid Flappers were christened 'The Four Horsewomen of The Algonquin', in acknowledgment of their morals. They were hunters. They were myth. They rode out.

She headlined *Everyday*, as another nervous flapper, in another play by Rachel Crothers. It played for 30 performances. Bad reviews. Didn't take. It closed.

In September 1922, she played nervous flapper, Mark 3, in *The Exciters* by Martin Brown.

And on her nights off, she was *being* a nervous kid flapper, acquiring an expensive taste for cigarettes, bourbon, sassy talk and sexual encounters of the non-lasting, unblessed-by-holy-church kind.

> *'My family warned me about men, but they never mentioned a word about women.'*

Tallulah asserted that she was a virginal virgin until she was seventeen and a 'technical virgin' until she was twenty. 'I had my share of necking. More than once I trembled on the brink of compliance.' She went out with men. She went out with women. She had crushes on unsuitable women – the happily married, shocked society girls, the relentlessly heterosexual. She had one-night stands with girls who 'came back' to visit her dressing-room after shows.

At a party in 1922, Tallulah was interrupted in the kitchen locked in a fervent snog with a woman on the kitchen table. She asked the uninvited third party for a handkerchief, fixed her make-up and sashayed out to the dance area. In Washington, Eugenia overheard one of her guests say 'Everyone knows her sister is a lesbian'. Eugenia, breaking up some ice for the cocktails, threw the ice pick at the blabbermouth. Tallulah said 'I don't care what they say as long as they talk about me.'

In 1921, Eugenia and Morton got an apartment on the West Side, next door to their best friends, Scott and Zelda Fitzgerald. Tallulah visited a lot and was particularly fond of Zelda, an old Southern friend. This was Zelda and Scott:

> *'Driving along the Corniche one evening, she said to her companion, "I think I'll turn off here" and had to be physically restrained from veering over a cliff."*

Another time she lay down in front of a parked car and said 'Scott, drive over me.' Fitzgerald had started the engine and had actually released the brake when someone slammed it on again.

At the audition with Barrymore, expectedly, he hit on Tallulah in his dressing room, making 'fervent little animal noises'. As she said to Margalo Gillmore later 'I hope you won't think me cheap. But I've allowed John Barrymore to kiss me.' Not cheap. No! But self-publicising? You bet! Barrymore asked her to be in his *Dr Jekyll and Mr Hyde* but she turned him down. 'I had no prejudices against informal alliances but felt no good should come of trying to blend business with pleasure'. Ah, Mother Theresa, ah Pope Joan. Tallulah did however, develop a prejudice with regards to the size of Mr Barrymore's penis. It was, reputedly, impressive and Tallulah in future penile discussions with all walks of life, hoped that other men were 'hung like Barrymore'. A size Queen, then.

In Zoe Akins' *Footloose*, playing Rose de Brissac at The Greenwich Theater, Burns Mantle (don't you just love the name?) of the *Evening Mail* wrote 'Tallulah is a promising young ingénue, able to inject a telling realism in a difficult role' The injection may well have come from her grief at the death of Granddaddy. Her Grandmamma wrote to her, 'Precious heart, be unselfish and do as many little acts of kindness as possible, and it will in return bring joy to you.'

It seems she did. Like most appalling teenagers who surl and sneer and lour about, she was bottomlessly kind and generous – sending flowers and cards and notes to her friends as they opened in shows, giving away her few possessions at the drop of a trouser and being endearingly sweet to all old people.

On 30 April 1921, Tallulah participated, with an Algonquin crowd consisting of, among others, Dorothy Parker, Ring Lardner, Roberts Benchley and Sherwood and George Kaufmann in a 'one-off anonymous entertainment' at the 39th Street Theater, thrillingly titled *No, Sirree!* She appeared in the sketch 'He Who Gets Flapped', a twenties take on Ostrovsky's *He Who Gets Slapped.*

In August 1922, she was in *Her Temporary Husband* at the Frazee Theater. Written by Edward A. Paulton [Who?] and directed and produced by H. Frazee. It played for 92 performances. She opened another Rachel Crothers-written, Mary Kirkpatrick-produced Oeuvre *Everyday* at The Bijou Theater, on the 16 November 1921. Not a huge box-office or critical success, it closed after 30 performances.

Tallulah is known about town but she isn't yet a big, unassailable star. This comment from a critic; 'She had a lot of silly friends in the theatre who gave her an ovation before she had done a thing ... a real case of SAVE ME FROM MY FRIENDS!' She has a following but she isn't doing solid, lasting work. She is in danger of sinking without trace, a pleasure boat on the sparkling sea for just the one or two summers.

She was also taking cocaine. This, in the 1920's, was called, affectionately and so imaginatively, 'Snow' – an invitation thus 'Will You Come To My Snow Ball?' meant 'we've got drugs'. It was $50 dollars an ounce and we just know that Tallulah was not the sort of girl to say 'I don't, thank you very much.' When too poor to buy any cocaine, rumour has it that she crushed up aspirin and sniffed a line of that. Now *that* must have hurt but was probably very good for a hangover. When high as a kite, she started performing her cartwheels at coke parties, and as it took as a party trick, performing cartwheels without any pants on. Estelle Winwood fought a rearguard action against Tallulah's excesses by frisking her occasionally and going through her bag and throwing her drugs down the loo. But as Tallulah said 'Cocaine isn't habit-forming. I should know – I've been taking it for years!'

Halfway through the run of *Nice People*, Tallulah had started sharing the apartment of rich girl Bijou Martin, daughter of opera star Ricardo Martin. Bijou taught her advanced drunkenness and introduced her to visiting Brit Poshingtons – Noel Coward, Geoffrey Holmesdale and Jeffrey John Archer Amherst, the fifth Earl Of Amherst. Among the British crowd was Napier George Henry Sturt Alington, third baron of Alington. He was twenty-four, he was nicknamed Naps, he was bisexual, sexy, exotic – and trouble. His friend Cecil Beaton described him as 'a tired boy in appearance, essentially young, with the willowy figure of a bantamweight champion, a neat head covered with a cap of silken hair, pale, far-seeing eyes and full negroid lips.' Dish of Dish Hall, in fact. He was gorgeous, he was unobtainable. Tallulah fell for him like a pack of playing cards. They were inseparable for the winter of 1922, Tallulah ungluing only on 22 December 1922 to appear in *Danger* by Cosmo Hamilton at the 39th Street Theater, replacing Kathlene McDonnell for 79 performances.

Here, our little pleasure boat shifts and bobs to face another direction. A wind of change blows ... and that wind points the prow towards England.

Bijou Martin, Estelle Winwood and Tallulah had taken to mysticism. For Tallulah, with Aunt Louise before her, it ran in the family. The Mystic Flavour of That Month was Evangeline Adams, from Scotland, who lived in a Fuck-Off Apartment on Riverside Drive. She had a catholic approach to fortune-telling, moving through tarot, astrology, to random opening of the bible ... by pricking it with a spiritually-channelled pin. Estelle was dealt the frightening snake card. Estelle handed it right back. Tallulah's first pinprick got 'Jezebel' [And they say there's nothing in it]. Estelle knew her bible – Jezebel gets thrown to the dogs, but Tallulah knew that she got to fool around with Top-notch Biblical Glitterati before! Evangeline did, however, come up with this prophesy 'Your future is in England. You must go there at once – even if you have to swim.'

Well, Aunt Marie had always averred that they had strong British roots. Grandmamma's stationery had always borne a *royal* crest. Tallulah knew that there were *no* beautiful women in London. Naps was now in England. Her career wasn't soaring quite as she'd hoped. She was getting work, but it wasn't *top* work.

When she opened in *The Exciters*, she was playing yet another version of herself – the febrile, chain-smoking, hootch-hurling flapper. *Vanity Fair* referred to her as 'the world's most subtly amusing imitator of Ethel Barrymore.' We can see that doesn't imply *range, staying power*, or *awed respect*. Although one review had her as 'ripe and gorgeous ... makes you believe she is going far ... ', Burns Mantle noted 'She is a gifted young woman upon whose shoulders we fear success is weighing a little heavily. She looks tired and a bit fed up with her work.'

Remember, the little thing is only nineteen. She has come a long way in a very short time. Her support has been slender. No mother or father to feed her roast dinners and love. No drama school training to fall back on. She is fuelled purely by youth, adrenalin, excitement and illegal substances. She is

Kate Moss. She is Liza Minnelli. She is Carrie Fisher. She should be doing six weeks in The Betty Ford Clinic. But, as Thoroughly Modern Millie trills 'This is nineteen *twenty-two*!' and everything today is thoroughly crazy.

Frank Crowninshields throws another of his legendary parties. Charles Cochran, English theatrical impresario, is there. Estelle Winwood knows him, introduces him to Tallulah. He has heard about her in his *Vanity Fair* – she's the one who does fantastic impersonations of Ethel Barrymore! Yes, she is! Here comes one now! He loves it! Can he have her details? But of course! He returns to England with her main calling card, a glamour photograph of her with the cleaning fluid glossy hair, the smouldering eyes, the sexy mouth.

Perhaps nothing will come of it. That's ShowBiz.

Six weeks later, Cochran sends a dream cable: POSSIBLE ENGAGEMENT WITH GERALD DU MAURIER IN ABOUT EIGHT WEEKS. Sir Gerald Du Maurier is the best director/manager in London! Gladys Cooper swears by him! He has co-written a play with Viola Tree, which has a good part ... 'an American girl, somewhat of a siren and in one scene has to dance'. The girl is stunning-looking. Cochran thinks Tallulah would be 'the goods' and has told Sir Gerald so. Was she interested?

Was she interested?!

Cochran promised to pay expenses if she would get herself over to England. Her salary would be half what she got in New York. Tallulah booked a passage on the *Majestic* and started looking about for the money. Her father, ever the supportive, thought that Cochran should have paid up front. So no luck there. Also, he was strapped for cash because he was paying for Eugenia's divorce from Morton Hoyt. She asked around at The Algonquin for money for her trip. Nothing. Finally, she borrowed the $1,000 off Colonel Coleman, DuPont, friend of her father, a Congressman, rich, and clearly, A Soft Touch.

Tallulah cabled she would come. Cochran cabled back: 'TERRIBLY SORRY. DU MAURIER'S PLANS CHANGED'. She cabled back: 'I'M

COMING ANYHOW!' He replied with 'DON'T. THERE'S A DEPRESSION HERE. IT'S VERY BAD.'

Tallulah decided to pretend that she never got the last cable. She had the passage fare. She was going.

In New York Harbour, she was given a magnificent farewell. She had, of course, forgotten to pack a coat. And she had given away her last decent one to a fan. Estelle took off her own mink. Gave it to Tallulah. [I want a friend like Estelle.] Then, think *Now Voyager* – a ship's horn sounds, a cloud of steam, and the proud ship is dragged by its little tugs out into the mighty ocean. She's bound for England, me Hearties.

TALLULAH IN 'THE CREAKING CHAIR', WRITTEN BY THE GLORIOUSLY
NAMED EDWARD KNOBLOCK

We have escaped by the luckiest chance ...

The gods in heaven it's plain to see
Are green with jealousy about you and me
we have escaped by the luckiest chance so
let's have fun, let's play, let's dance ...[10]

David Mamet, in *True and False: Heresy and Common Sense for The Actor*, begins with this news: 'My closest friends, my intimate companions, have always been actors. My beloved wife is an actor. My extended family consists of the actors I have grown-up, worked, lived and aged with. I have been, for many years, part of various theatre companies, any one of which in its healthy state more nearly resembles a perfect community than any other group that I have encountered.'

In 1922, a nineteen year old girl, an actress, sets off from America alone, to cross the Atlantic for London, England. She has a job that might or might not materialise. She knows one person in England – Naps Alington. She has met Charles Cochran, once.

She passed the long days at sea having fun, forgetting she has no money and no secure job, and dancing. The important dance at that time was the Charleston, described by a Disgusted Of Tunbridge Wells letter-writer in the *Daily Mail* of that time as so: 'With the addition of war paint and feathers, the Charleston would rival the antics of a tribe of savages. Let us have dances to conform with our standards of civilisation.'

When she was a few days away from Southampton, she cabled Cochran that she was coming. He said he would meet her. The *Majestic* docked at

Southampton, she took the train to London. Cochran met her at Paddington. He booked her into The Ritz Hotel and the next day he and his wife spent their time planning her next step. They decided on the big fat lie that the cable calling off the London gig, had never got to her, and Cochran would try to talk du Maurier into taking her on.

The theatre world is Mamet's 'perfect community' because it has to be. For it to work, a theatre company has to become an instant family, a family that has to function for the length of time the show goes on, long or short. Its members have to find their place as mother, father, favoured child, firstborn, second child, family fool, kind auntie, black sheep uncle – immediately. Some companies are dysfunctional, some are harmonious dynasties, some are The Carringtons, some The Colbys, a few are The March family, one or two are The Addams Family and some are The Borgias. Everyone starts off trying to be The Waltons and usually settles for a version of the very family they sprung from, finding their own dysfunctional niche in a Back and Onstage Scenario.

Tallulah, in New York, had been the motherless, adopted foundling. In London, she was accepted as the same. Perdita. She was immediately swept into the warm, generous embrace of British Theatre. Cochran took her along to Wyndham's to watch Gerald du Maurier in *Bulldog Drummond*. He was fifty, but still doing matinee idol stuff. This is the line-up; du Maurier, Leslie Howard, George Sanders, Cary Grant, David Niven, George Clooney. du Maurier was a noted skirt-chaser. Tallulah went backstage after the show to say, a) Gerald, you were *wonderful*, b) I love you and, c) Here I am. Give me my Job. Tallulah had made a long sea crossing, was wearing a crumpled coat and indifferent hat. Not the way to do it. du Maurier had given the part of Maxine, the flapper to someone else. Damn!

What to do? Cochran was an impresario and a business man. Unless he got Tallulah the Maxine part, he would be out of pocket on a one-way fare from New York. He advised her to meet du Maurier when he hadn't just come off stage, when he wasn't surrounded by adoring stage-goers. She arrived hatless. His daughter Daphne du Maurier, a novelist, a romantic, a bisexual, was introduced to Tallulah. Daphne, who would go on to create the impetuous Lady

Dona St Columb in *Frenchman's Creek*, the terrifying Mrs Danvers in *Rebecca* and brave, naughty, crippled Honor Harris in *The King's General*, said 'Daddy, this is quite the most beautiful girl I've seen in my life!' By this time, Gerald was in agreement with his daughter. He signed her up as Maxine for £30 a week, a third of the original actress's fee, but then, she was retained on full salary for the run in case Tallulah proved a turkey. The play previewed in two weeks.

Tallulah hadn't seen or heard from Naps Alington since he had returned to England. She therefore resolved to be elegant but cool; polite, but distant. He called at her hotel looking gorgeous, dangerous and ... with a Pekinese puppy. Naps was living with Lord Latham, a theatrical designer and rich guy. A married man. But these two were soul sisters. Elegance, coolness, politeness and distance went for nought. They called the dog Napoleon. Naps and Tallulah spent the afternoon in bed making love; Napoleon spent the afternoon on the carpet making puddles.

The London equivalent of the Kid Flappers were known as Bright Young Things. They lunched and dined at The Ivy and they drank cocktails all day and fucked virtual strangers in uncomfortable, but cool, outdoor locations about the metropolis.

Naps introduced her to that band of society which is awash with folks who don't have to earn a living but want to be artists – the upper class of Old England. Daddy Will got a letter about her seeing The Yorks in a minor royals procession; 'The people rode in Golden Coaches more beautiful than in Fairy Tales. Daddy dear, having a King and Queen makes *such* a difference!' She met Olga Lynn, a concert singer who she would soon go and live with. She met all the bisexuals, gays and lesbians who ran theatre and the London social scene. Tallulah was whisked into The Bright Young Things as briskly as a speckled egg into an omelette. She and Naps went to The Bright Young Things Costume Ball as twin brothers from the Court of Louis Quatorze, wearing powder-blue satin knee breeches tight in all the right places. She had only to say loudly in her best Southern drawl at the right moment 'It's fine for you, Naps, but how do *I* pee?' to go down as witty, exotic and amusing.

With a stonking hangover, Tallulah started rehearsals for *The Dancers*. Now, you will be gagging for this play to be revived when I tell you that it was a melodrama in four acts, about two young girls who are so mad about the Charleston that it takes over their lives. Maxine (Tallulah's character) actually exploits her acumen at the dance to go on and become a famous ballerina [Oh come *on* – the two disciplines *are* practically *the same*], while the English girl (played by Audry Carten) falls for her dance partner, gets up the duff and has to commit suicide. The Earl of Cheveley (the Gerald du Maurier role), in open shirt and flared riding breeches, takes Maxine, dressed in a white buckskin Native American tunic, with full Warbonnet of white feathers, but with her hair showing at the back, to a Wild West Saloon. He buys her a cocktail [like you do in frontier saloons] and this naturally makes her perform a sort of Oglala-Sioux Charleston! Maxine's story is unfolded in acts one and four; Audry's in two and three.

Gerald directed this drama classic. Tallulah, her body her temple, gave up smoking for a *full week* so she would not be puffed after the half-breed dance. Gerald's directing style was taking his actresses to lunch, buying them presents, telling them they were brilliant and generally getting them to fall in love with him. Works for me. And Tallulah. And Audry.

The play opened at Wyndham's on 15th February, 1923. Some churlish critics labelled the play 'far-fetched'. When Tallulah performed her hybrid dance, it was received in awed silence. She retired to her dressing room to cry, and contemplate another career choice. But at the end of each act, the audience stamped and yelled and clapped. At curtain call, flowers rained down from the balcony. Anton Dolin in the *Daily Sketch* remarked of Tallulah 'She could have gone through any modern ballet and not even been out of breath at the end.' Hannen Swaffer in the *Daily Express* said 'Tallulah is the essence of sophistication, she gives electric shocks! Sex oozes from her eyes! She is daring and friendly and rude and nice, and all at once!' Again, her reviews were about her sexiness, not her acting. She was still playing herself. The chances of her settling down quietly and exploring her craft and turning into Peggy Ashcroft were slim. J. C. Trewin, theatre historian, recorded 'A smouldering, pouting young woman, with a voice like hot honey and milk and a face like an angry flower, the play could not have mattered less. She had acted herself into a cult.'

Tallulah had made it in London. The show settled in for a long run. She took to going out for supper after her exit in Act One, returning just before curtain-up in Act Four, when her character returned. She became a favourite icon of a phenomenon called 'The Gallery Girls'. While the stalls and boxes and royal circle of Wyndham's were filled with The Posh and The Rich, in evening dress, tie and tails, furs, the works ... up in the upper circle and the gallery, in the cheapest seats, where the stage was a long, long way away, both in actual distance and in aspirations, were the most ardent fans of theatre. The majority of these fans were London working class, who queued relentlessly for tickets ,who sat on hard wood benches to see theatre, and to have long-distance, shouty, weepy crushes on their performer of choice. Tallulah. They copied her every gesture. Grafted Tallulah's Southern drawl onto their Cockney intonations, added 'Darling' to their sentences. They would come night after night, so they knew the play, knew when Tallulah was on and rush out after her First Act exit to catch her going off for supper, leave when she was offstage or just sit chatting or having a bit of a singsong in the auditorium while the rest of the melodrama spooled through, ready to roar and cheer when she came back.

One night she suddenly decided, on a whim, to cut her hair into a bob, which made Cochran apoplectic and Gerald threaten to fire her. Tallulah said 'Go Ahead then, I don't Care!' and went on stage to experience a profound silence, an Arctic drop in audience temperature. She was terrified. Then suddenly, The Gallery Girls went for it. Bobbed hair was *In*. The Girls started cutting their own hair in the theatre *during the performance!* Instead of flowers thrown, it was hanks of hair. Arnold Bennett [can *your* mind put him together with Tallulah in the same history zone?] wrote at the time:

> *'At 2pm you see girls, girls, girls in seated queues at the pit and gallery doors of the theatre. They are a mysterious lot, these stalwarts of the cult. They seem to belong to the clerk class, but they cannot be clerks, typists, shop assistants, trottins, for such people don't – can't – take a day and a half off whenever 'Tallulah'*

opens. What manner of girls are they, then? Only a statistical individual enquiry could answer the question. All one can say is that they are bright, youthful, challenging, proud of themselves and apparently happy. It is certain that they boast afterwards to their friends about the number of hours they waited for the thrill of beholding their idol, and those who have waited the longest become heroines to their envious acquaintances!'

Well, they are *Fans*, Arnold. They are the people who go and see *Cats*, *Les Miserables*, *Phantom Of The Opera*, *The Sound Of Music* hundreds of times. Who travel the country to see Barry Manilow; In Concert. Who fainted at The Beatles. Whose inert bodies are passed over the heads of crowds from bouncer to bouncer at every rock concert. Who stand outside Take That's Mums' houses. Who found Fan Clubs. Who stand staring at Michael Jackson's curtained hotel window all night. Seekers after Safe Excitement. Contained Thrills. Non-participating, one-sided love affairs which won't break their hearts.

And specifically in this instance, *Lesbian* fans. They are having long-distance, safe, unreciprocated *Lesbian Crushes*, Arnold. Just like Tallulah for Sister Ignatius, for Nazimova, for Ethel Barrymore.

As Tallulah said 'If I'd dashed on stage and started eating the props, they'd have followed suit.'

The Dancers was to run for 344 performances. In an indifferent play, with two-dimensional characters, you get bored. Then the production is vulnerable to two things; Practical Joking and Corpsing. Sir Gerald was a relentless practical joker, in the interfering with anything you might have to eat on stage way, whoopee cushions to produce loud farts during serious emotional scenes, spookily moving chairs and comedy props. This sort of palaver made him helpless with laughter. Of course, Tallulah and Audry, now close friends, could not but retaliate. They organised Sir Gerald a very late-night, massed serenade in his garden; they organised the funeral arrangements for several living members of *The Dancers* cast and crew; they telephoned halves of loving couples anonymously to reveal the details of many imaginary steamy romances being pursued by the other half. They spent the play trying to corpse each other. Given the costumes and the plot, this cannot have been difficult.

Tallulah started a run of the usual media coverage where all the articles say the same − young, new, beautiful, talented, American. Her looks got her on the cover of all magazines, particularly image leader *The Tatler*. She looked gorgeous, with her newly bobbed hair establishing a very modern 'flapper' look.

Tallulah, who had moved from The Ritz into a small flat organised by Naps, was asked to move in with Olga Lynn. Olga was older than Tallulah, a bit Mrs Tiggy-Winkle in looks and with a tuneful but small singing voice. Unable to fill opera houses with a wall of sound, she made her dosh by singing at influential smaller concert halls and socially-okay drawing rooms. She was well read, connected, popular, amusing and loaded. Tallulah could perform cartwheels and was young and sexy. So it was a meeting of souls. Olga had a spiffy house in Catherine Street, which, as everyone with an A to Z of London knows, was handily situated off the Aldwych, within spitting distance of Wyndham's and in the heart of British Theatre Land. Get legless in any socially accepted part of London and you could get home. Olga had servants. 'To be a friend of Olga's is a liberal education in *Who's Who and What's What*', wrote Percy Colson.

Tallulah wrote to Daddy 'I live in a divine big house with Olga Lynn who is the most divine woman and has been a great friend to me. She is much older but everyone worships her and she has a lot of influence in every direction.' As we will see, it was a love match.

Such a popular success was *The Dancers* that, two months into the run, when Gerald du Maurier took two weeks off and the management brought in an understudy, it had no adverse effect on box-office takings. The bulk of the audience came to see Tallulah and when she was off-stage, management could have sent on a dog in a frock and got away with it. When Gerald came back, bronzed and refreshed, Tallulah decided *she* should have two weeks off. This mutiny in the ranks terrified Gerald, who had just upped ticket prices and was wary of losing his Main Drawing Attraction. He refused her leave.

TALLULAH WITH HER LION
CUB WINSTON CHURCHILL.
WHEN ASKED WHAT
WOULD HAPPEN WHEN HE
GOT BIGGER, TALLULAH
REPLIED, 'I'LL ASK FOR A
BIGGER DRESSING-ROOM'

She said she was going anyway. He magnanimously offered her a rise in salary to what it should have been anyway. She told him to put his money where the sun never shines. Finally his co-writer, Viola Tree, announced that she and Olga Lynn were taking Tallulah with them to Venice. So he could put that in his flared breeches. Of course, we know the perils of women travelling abroad alone. The three of them, simpering gentler sex as they were, had to have a man to protect them. They chose Sir Guy Francis Laking, nineteen, alcoholic and as Tallulah put it, 'so frail, if he came he would blow himself off the face of the earth!'

'In Venezia, Venezia, you step in the street and get wetsia'. The fabulous foursome stayed with The Cole Porters. Their lavender marriage was riding out a rough patch, probably brought upon by those little things that can irritate you in marriage – the husband was having a passionate fling with Monty Woolley, an actor, and both of them were up for ordering in black stud room service, and soliciting rough trade and bringing it back to the house. The Porter couple ran their house like a hotel for Americans passing through Venice, with Cole as a sort of insufferably rude, snobbish Basil Fawlty. The four from London fitted right in. Tallulah gondola'd about, without a hat, in the 106 degree temperature and came down with sunstroke. She had a few days lying down in a shady room wanting to die, then up for more Porter Establishment Gentle Fun. They went back to London by that clever dodge route that takes in Paris, where her two adoring older women fans helped her to shop at Chez Molyneux for dresses and silk lounging pyjamas. [Why don't *I* meet these people? Too busy writing biographies.]

Tallulah and Olga returned to Catherine Street. Here, Tallulah was protected from the more insistent of The Gallery Girls' attention. But, in what sounds like older lover giving younger a good time, Tallulah got her own personal maid and wild, wild parties after every show. She went back into *The Dancers*, but at the increased salary du Maurier had offered to keep her out of Venice. Her reappearance sent the play's takings into cyberspace, and it ran and ran ...

Still only twenty, Tallulah, feted and petted, was developing a low boredom and tolerance threshold and an ability both to attract and then alienate people. She was honest and spontaneous. She was libidinous and friendly. She was amusing and shocking. 'I can say shit, dahling, I'm a lady.'

Of course, someone who is a hit in a West End Play gets offered all sort of toshy roles. Tallulah didn't turn them down flat, she just kept agreeing to do them for ever increasing outrageous salaries. Eventually, her bluff was called, and she had to agree to do *Conchita* by Edward Knoblock for £200 a week, at The Queen's Theatre. She would be star, with above title billing. She thought the playwright's name very funny. She did it as a joke.

It was. Conchita was a Cuban girl running a hotel in Havana for a wealthy politician. We don't need to go any further do we? She was Cuban, therefore she was fiery, passionate, hot-blooded and showed a lot of cleavage. He was a wealthy Cuban politician, therefore he was slippery, unreliable and – well – generally your Johnny Foreigner. The appropriately named Edward Knoblock clearly had writer's integrity and followed the old dictum 'only write about what you know'. It opened on 19th March 1924 and it was a *stinker*. Tallulah had decided, for artistic reasons, (nothing to do with inability!) not to go for a Cuban accent. She got into her character by wearing a long black wig. And – I've been saving this – the plot involved – a Monkey! Tallulah and the monkey did not get on (too alike), he wrenched her black wig (and entire character) off her head and pitched it into the orchestra pit. Tallulah retaliated by shaking the monkey and performing her famous cartwheels, such a spectacle as you might see any day in any hotel in downtown Havana. Amazingly, the audience could not see this piece as anything but a comedy. A percipient critic wrote 'Tallulah never gave the impression of being the least bit Spanish'. Tallulah rode it out, the boos, the walk-outs, even disguising herself and her maid and infiltrating the crowd outside the theatre with mutterings about 'that god-awful play and that awful Bankhead woman.' It closed after 37 performances. She celebrated its early demise at Ciro's restaurant, pouring a pint of beer over Gladys Cooper's head for calling the play 'crap'. You can diss yourself but nobody else better diss you too. The monkey returned to zoo work.

In later years, Tallulah referred to *Conchita* as 'one of the all-time clinkers'. While she soldiered on in its brief run she will have suffered horribly. Nobody wants to be in a flop, particularly a twenty year old Space Cadet.

A break came with her next job. *This Marriage* at the Comedy had no monkeys, and Herbert Marshall and Cathleen Nesbitt as co-stars. An eternal triangle play, *This Marriage* was terribly *modern* in that the wife was in favour of open marriage, only to be disconcerted by her husband embracing the concept and a mistress wholeheartedly. Tallulah was the mistress and had sassy, wise, *modern* aphorisms to deliver, which were much applauded by The Gallery Girls. Cathleen Nesbitt was a young wife and mother at the time, She and Tallulah got on (there had been a '*you* have the best dressing room' 'no *you* have the best dressing room' exchange which had gone *terribly* well) and so, while onstage all was sophisticated and urbane, backstage was A Baby-Worshipping Zone, with Cathleen breastfeeding and Tallulah besotting. 'The baby was much more interesting than anything we did or said on stage', said Tallulah. The play ran for 53 performances. The baby must now be in his seventies. *Ars Longa, Vita Brevis*.

After *This Marriage* closed, Tallulah let it be known that she was taking some time out to find work she *really* wanted to do. Yes, she was out of work. She passed her time doing what every out of work actor does. She went in for healthy, self-improving, meditational retreats. No, okay, she spent time digging into Cathleen Nesbitt's old affair with Rupert Brooke to assess how much of a gay he really was. Her friend from *The Dancers*, Audry Carten, after a promising start, had retired from the stage. She could not handle the pressure. She was twenty-three. Along with Audry and her brother Kenneth, an inky schoolboy, Tallulah hung out, resting. She went to watch Kenneth compete in the Under Sixteen All-England Tennis Championships, in the Barbra Streisand watching Agassi role: 'Hit it! Hit it, you son of a bitch!' Kenneth won. Tallulah was beside herself with pride. The three of them went to the movies every Sunday night. Kenneth and Tallulah were big cry buckets. She hung out with Sir Guy Francis Laking, who lisped and made her laugh. He was a gossip, motorist and fixer. She jauntered off to Brighton in his fast car, breaking down a lot. On Saturday nights, Tallulah and friends drank and played games at home – well, Olga Lynn's home. They played that old reliable wrecker, *Truth*. Tears were spilt. Friendships ruined. Relationships tainted forever.

Then, oh joy of joys, she got a cable saying Daddy was coming over to London on business. Well, she wanted to impress him, so when she was offered that enduring classic *The Creaking Chair*, she accepted with alacrity. *The Creaking Chair* was written by our old friend, Edward Knoblock. Drawing once again from the dictum 'write from *experience*', this oeuvre was a thriller about a crippled Egyptologist. Tallulah played his mysterious wife. Don't those crippled Egyptologists *always* marry mysterious women?

Daddy arrived. Tallulah on Best Behaviour. Aunt Marie, ever the archivist and family cuttings repository, wrote asking for newspaper clippings of Tallulah's successes. Tallulah was careful to never quite get round to sending them. The newspapers were full of steamy little pieces of gossip about her goings-on. Daddy did not get to see them.

She attended a white-tie, big cheese dinner at The Savoy. Those present included Lords Birkenhead, Balfour, Beaverbrook; Ladies Manners and Tree. Daddy drank a toast to International Peace in this wise: 'American women are the most beautiful women in the world. And now I can see why, because they're descended from the English and the Irish.' So *there* India, France, Sweden, Africa, South America – *Cuba.*

Tallulah was *behaving*: Not saying to Peers of the Realm with their wives, staring at her across a crowded restaurant, 'Don't you recognise me with my clothes on?' Not emptying pints of best bitter over Grande Dames de Theatre. Not answering the door at Catherine Street stark naked. Not turning cartwheels knickerless in late night bars. Daddy was invited round to the house in Catherine Street. All was decorum. All was politesse. We all know those parental visits, don't we? Low-key on the bedroom arrangements, watch the content of the bookshelves, mention *straight* couples and heterosexuality a lot as if it's *the norm*. Daddy somehow didn't get to see *The Creaking Chair*, but he did see Tallulah's impersonation of Sarah Bernhardt, her party piece of the time. It was rumoured to make grown men cry.
The Creaking Chair got awful reviews. Edward Knoblock, taking a bow on press night was booed. Tallulah was crucified in a cartoon as a cottage-loaf set on spindly legs. She sued. She and co-star Nigel Bruce managed to turn the whole thing round by sending up the creaky whodunnit formula and hokey lines. It ran for 235 sell-out nights and because of a tough Aubrey Smith, who as manager, put Tallulah on a Draconian allowance, thus forcing her to save, she was able to buy a little car. A Talbot Coupe. Green and cream colour scheme. She studied, took driving lessons and would have been a *terrific* driver, had she had any sense of direction. Getting from Catherine Street to the Comedy was beyond her, unless she flagged down and followed a cab.

She was a success. She was brave. She was outrageous. She had a huge dykey following. But she didn't want to be known as a lesbian. She was scared of the butches in male drag who slouched about London. But she gave good riposte:

'I couldn't possibly go to Lady ———— for the weekend. I'm so bloody tired of three in a bed.'

'I'm sick to death of all those royal lesbians following me around'

'I don't know who I am, Dahling. I've tried several varieties of sex. The conventional position makes me claustrophobic. And the others either give me a stiff neck or lockjaw.'

There was no reliable contraception. She slept with men. She had abortions. She gave good rumour. Stories circulated that she had ten abortions in ten months, that the Prince Of Wales *himself* donated a pint of his royal blood for one of her little operations, that she would 'never go back to that place again. They aborted me with rusty nails and old razor blades.'

She was probably hopelessly unclued up about contraception, sex, sexuality. She was fucking without context, without perspective.

Cecil Beaton, in his diaries, comments on a night at the Tower restaurant;

'Tallulah arrived late, went to every table and was quick-witted at each. She has developed her personality to such an extent that she always seems natural, but it is only acting.'

How very exhausting for her. She had to be 'On' all the time. She had thousands of acquaintances, but few friends. Mrs Pat Campbell said:

'Tallulah is always skating on thin ice. Everyone wants to be there when it breaks.'

She was right. Unkind. But right.

The TATLER

Vol. CXVII. No. 1523. London, September 3, 1930   POSTAGE: Inland, 2d.; Canada and Newfoundland, 1½d.; Foreign, 4d.   Price One Shilling

"LAUGHTER HOLDING BOTH HIS SIDES!"

A SCENE IN "LET US BE GAY" AT THE LYRIC

Mr. Francis Lister as Townley Town, the "professional guest," Mr. Arthur Margetson as Bob Brown, whose own divorced Kitty (Miss Tallulah Bankhead) is co-opted by old Mrs. Boucicault (Miss Helen Haye) to vamp her own ex-husband, and so save an amorous damsel named Deirdre from making a fool of herself. It ends up with Bob and Kitty deciding to get married again. The play is fully dealt with in The Passing Shows pages in this issue

TALLULAH AS KITTY IN 'LET US BE GAY'

Beautiful, wild, wilful and wearily discontented

> *Oh how weary I am of our rakish friends!*
> *How tired I am of rich and dissolute men!*
> *How fatigued I am with beautiful and powdered women!*
> *Small wonder I am ardent and wilful!*
> *Small wonder London society is agog with my*
> *outrageous pranks!*[11]

In the next few years, television will be invented, Scott Fitzgerald will write *The Great Gatsby*, James Joyce will write *Ulysses*, Hitler, *Mein Kampf* and T.S. Eliot, *The Waste Land*. Mussolini will form a government in Italy, there will be the first labour government in England with Ramsey Macdonald as Prime Minister. The Ottoman empire will end. In the divvying-up, Palestine, Transjordan and Iraq will go to Britain and Syria to France. Chiang Kai-shek will set about unifying China. The BBC will be founded. The ionosphere will be discovered. The British General Strike will last nine days. The US Economy will boom, then crash. Ravel will compose *Bolero* – ready for Torvil and Dean. Penicillin will be discovered. Saccho and Vanzetti will be strapped up and executed. Women over twenty-one will be enfranchised in the USA. Lenin will die. The Red Army will develop in the USSR.

But all that needn't bother *us*.

Somerset Maugham had written *Rain*. It was a massive hit in America, but Jeanne Engels, starring as tragic tough tart Sadie Thompson, didn't want to flog across the Pond to play it in England. Basil Dean, Producer and Man-In-Dire-Financial-Straits, decided that Tallulah might be just perfect for the lead role. 'Although comparitively inexperienced for such a big emotional part, she would be an undoubted box-office attraction.'

Sadie Thompson carried the play. She had a broad palette of emotions and she didn't perform cartwheels. Tallulah also decided she was perfect for the role. The only fly in the ointment was that some fool in the Contracts Department had given Somerset Maugham casting approval. As if a *playwright* has any idea about casting his own play!

Talks began. Tallulah started learning her lines and agreed to take a salary of £30 per week (she was sharp enough to know it was *art* and she needed a big *serious* part to move forward into a respectable strata of casting) but it was a substantial cut in her earnings. She agreed to go and see Jeanne Engels in the part, then come back to England to start rehearsing. But only if Somerset Maugham agreed to her. Basil Dean went off first to set things up, Tallulah caught the *Berengaria*. Dean was playing a close, cautious game. Tallulah was playing – well, Tallulah. While Dean tiptoed around the notedly-difficult Maugham, Tallulah steamed right in like the *Berengaria* to force a decision out of him. Maugham had no opinion of Tallulah. She followed him to Washington, where she stayed with Daddy and went to see Engels in the show. She loved the performance, catching it again in Pittsburgh. Sadly, as she did when she took over from Constance Binney in *39 East*, Tallulah set to copying Engels' nuances, stresses, the whole performance's outer shell, without knowing how to discover her *own* path through the motivational forest. She tried to convince Maugham with girlish enthusiasm, that she was the only one for the part. It came across as aggression. Dean came back to London on the *Aquitania* with Maugham, wisely deciding that Tallulah should sail on *another* ship.

Back in London, the production, with Tallulah, got to first run-through stage before Maugham saw it. This was a dodgy, 'get-the-writer-on-the-star's-side' ploy, because first run-throughs are usually as appealing as drinking bleach. The writer wants his/her genius to shine through immediately, no matter how experienced he/she is, the actors are trying to remember their newly-learned lines and *where* the director said to put that glass of whiskey in the argument scene. Maugham watched with an expression of distaste, lips pursed like a cat's bum. Tallulah thought she gave the performance of her life. Maugham withheld casting approval. He said she had 'no personality'.

It is horribly painful for everybody, this type of stand-off. Fragile Egos crash to the ground. Insecurities bounce off the walls. You put your armour on. Tallulah chose this as *her* reason of choice: 'One of the curses of my gift for mimicry is that unconsciously I will blink if my opponent blinks, lisp if he lisps.' Maugham had a stonker of a stutter. 'I have a suspicion that I may have imitated Maugham's stutter.' It is a good, rather elegant excuse. But the use of 'opponent' is interesting. She probably knew, in her heart-of-performer's-heart, that what she had mimicked was actually Engel's performance, and what Maugham labelled 'no personality' was an almost kind misnomer for 'no technique'. He sent her a cheque for £100, which seems to me a sweet, if stupid, gesture. She sent it back. She should have taken it and gone out of town for a jaunt on it. Then she would have missed the news that, a few days later, Maugham approved an Anglo-Norwegian actress, Olga Lindo, as Sadie.

Everybody has one silly suicide attempt. This was Tallulah's. Now in her own flat (what had gone wrong with the Olga set-up? *Not* life-partners?) she tried to kill herself with an overdose of aspirins. I'm no expert, but I *think* this doesn't work. Her suicide note read 'It ain't gonna rain no mo.' Ah Tallulah, leave 'em laughing. She didn't die. The Suicide Attempt was demoted to Cry For Help status.

Life went on. Noel Coward's new comedy, *Fallen Angels*, was set to open at The Globe on 21 April, with Edna Best and Margaret Bannermann as the two married women, Jane and Julia, getting drunk while their joint erstwhile lover fails to arrive. Fortune smiled … for Tallulah … not Margaret Bannermann, who had a nervous breakdown five nights before first preview. Coward begged Tallulah to take over so *he* wouldn't have a nervous breakdown too. She demanded, and got, £100 a week. She worked like a dog and on opening night, knew the text.

Coward describes what happened thus:

> *'It was described by a large section of the press as amoral, disgusting, vulgar, an insult to British Womanhood. It was of course none of these things. They might with truth have said that it was extremely slight and needed a stronger last act;*

they might, with equal truth and more kindness have said that it had an amusing situation, some very funny lines, two excellent parts for two good actresses, and was vastly entertaining to the public. It was, I am glad to say, a great success and was played brilliantly by Edna Best and Tallulah Bankhead. I cannot honestly regard it as one of my best comedies, but it is gay and lighthearted and British womanhood has been cheerfully insulted by it for almost a quarter of a century.'

So there. It was the first time Tallulah got to play comedy. On opening night, Coward had to wait ten minutes for *his* curtain call, while the house called for the two leads. Also on opening night, Tallulah altered the line 'Oh Lord, more rain' to 'My Gawd, *Rain!*' Love-fifteen (Ha! Somerset). Her Gallery Girls shrieked with approval. It made the newspapers next day.

The show ran for 158 nights. *Rain* with Miss Lindo in the lead, for a shorter run. Love-thirty.

Tallulah and Edna Best had a run-of-show affair. Both jokers, they would declare that they could not stand their co-star, then turn up for parties, all over each other like a rash. As with *The Dancers*, practical joking and corpsing set in. All the old ones; substituting the prop drink for *real* drink, hurling in offputting business, cartwheels, 'going up' during the other's long speeches. Tallulah started tinkering with the text: 'Sanders, bring in the coffee now' became 'Coffee, bring in the Sanders now'. Call me a playwright, therefore picky with a text, but is that *better*? I guess you had to be there.

The play was attracting a lot of media coverage, moral outrage and opprobrium. Tallulah, as usual, gave good copy: she claimed she was as large as a house because of the stage eating involved, and as everyone knew 'she was very partial to chocolate cake and *big* bananas.' She also bragged about her abortion count, making the critic James Agate apoplectic enough to denounce her as 'a joyless creature whose spiritual home is the gutter'. The *Daily Express* ran a campaign to close the play, spearheaded by Mrs Charles Hornibrook, a sort of Mary Whitehouse *de ses jours*, who had already picketed that old Eugene O'Neill filth and now went after Noel Coward. She attended the play, standing up when she could take no more moral corruption to denounce it, tremulously.

Here's a contemporary newspaper account of the incident. 'Mr Noel Coward's much-discussed play *Fallen Angels* was made the occasion of a protest by Miss Hornibrook, who had resigned her membership of the London Council for the Promotion Of Public Morality in view of her fellow members' dislike of public protests. At the end of the second act, she stood up in a box and began to speak out against the play, but her words were drowned by the orchestra, which began to play "I Want To Be Happy".'

In *Present Indicative*, his autobiography, Coward writes;

> '*With* Fallen Angels, On With The Dance, *and* The Vortex *all running at once, I was in an enviable position. Everyone but Somerset Maugham said that I was a second Somerset Maugham.*'

Love-forty ...

Somerset Maugham came to the show, took her out to lunch and called the show the best comedy performance he had ever seen. Tallulah said 'I have two things to say to you, and the second is "off".'

Game.

Tallulah's next role was in the stage adaptation of Michael Arlen's *The Green Hat*. Katherine Cornell opened as the lead in New York in September 1925, Tallulah as the lead opened in London at the same time. Iris March, the heroine of this noble tale, is a modern, febrile, wonderful scorner of society's fragile mores and double-standards who gets ostracised by every one of the stinkers she has embraced, wears green a lot and deals her fair-weather friends a lesson in life by crashing her yellow Hispano-Suiza into an oak tree at seventy miles an hour.

A sample of her lines : 'You've all got Alma Maters instead of minds, and Union Jacks instead of hearts'; 'I have never given myself in disdain, in desire, with disgust, with delight'. It is said of her, 'You are a woman with magic eyes and a soft white body that beats at my brains like a whip.' Oh, and the male lead was called Napier and organised swim parties.

Katherine Cornell said 'I had to work my way into Iris March. Tallulah was already there.'

Spookily enough, the New York version enjoyed greater critical success than the London production, which got mixed reviews. 'Miss Bankhead is more than ever inaudible. She brought all her husky charm to the part of Iris and acted pleasantly and competently without making one feel that the character could have moved in any mentionable circle', opined James Agate. Hannen Swaffer disagreed: 'Tallulah Bankhead is almost the most modern actress we have. She belongs to the semi-exclusive set of whom Michael Arlen writes. She has beauty and a shimmering sense of theatre. So she made Iris a most fascinating study. She has moved starwards in great strides during the last year. Her art saved *Fallen Angels* from dreariness; now she has succeeded in a part about which even Gladys Cooper felt nervous.'

A word about criticspeak. 'Shimmering sense of theatre' means 'I can't spot that her characterisation isn't centred', 'Gladys Cooper felt nervous' means 'Gladys Cooper turned it down', and 'most modern actress' means 'she can't project, but she gets her kit off'.

It didn't matter. It was a popular success. It ran at the Adelphi for 128 performances. The first night was attended by The Prince of Wales, Mrs Coates of Coates Cotton Empire, Gladys Cooper, Ladies Curzon, du Maurier and Milford Haven, Lords Tweedmuir and Alington ... You get the picture.

Appearing in her underwear for the 'soft white body' scene drove the Gallery Girls into a frenzy. The Gallery was a potent force in Theatre then. Their opinions, calls, rehearsed responses, were similar to football terrace chants today. The press and theatre managements paid attention to their opinions because they had 'Influence'. Fat Sophie, a legendary lesbian figure in male drag and a large black umbrella, was listened to even by Tallulah, probably because she was her most ardent fan. Pip, a mouthy gay, indulged in carefully-placed heckling. The little passages and back alleys around theatres in London, where the upper theatre sitters queued, had little stools (you got them from Woolworths or the Theatre), which kept your place in the queue. Straight groups barracked gay groups. It was all refreshingly familiar.

After *The Green Hat*, came *Scotch Mist*. At St Martin's this time, it was written and produced by Sir Patrick Hastings, and Godfrey Tearle was her co-star. It opened 26 January 1926. Tallulah played the sexually voracious wife of a respected British cabinet minister. It was an absolute turkey. The Gallery loved it (more cartwheels and underwear), and The *Morning Post* said '*Scotch Mist* is one of the worst plays I have ever seen'. The Bishop of London denounced the play as moral turpitude, and dear Mrs Hornibrook agreed. So, of course, everyone went to see what the fuss was all about. Thus a popular success. 117 performances.

By now, Tallulah had been in London for three years. She was twenty three. Time to put down roots. She signed a ninety-nine year lease on 1 Farm Street, Mayfair. Just off Berkeley Square. Very Smart Address. Handy for the Theatre. Basement, then two floors, central spiral staircase. Not huge. Almost a cottage. Tallulah spent £3,000 making it cosy, with white and gold repro Louis Quinze furniture, the bedroom colour scheme was rose pinks and gold and Marion Dorn rugs. Syrie Maugham sold her most of the furniture and fittings (she had a chi-chi shop in Duke street) and Naps and Francis Laking helped her style it. The policy was 'open house'. She tried to make a 'home' – but what *was* that to her? Servants: her long-time dresser/maid Elizabeth Lock moved in. Then Arthur and Florence Meredith, a cockney couple, hired mostly because of their authentic Dickensian look. But they couldn't get on with noise, all-night parties and refrigerators, and when Arthur put it to the 'either the refrigerator goes or we do', ultimatum, the refrigerator stayed. Better ice in your drinks than no fluff under your bed. They were replaced by John and Mary Underdown, who liked fridges and Tallulah ... and John could impersonate Francis Laking. The last person hired was Edie Smith, a working-class Gallery Girl for whom Tallulah had put in a good word, with Gordon Selfridge Junior, and who was working as bakeryasssistant at Selfridge's Food Hall. When Elizabeth Lock went off to nurse her sick mother, Edie answered Tallulah's distress rocket. As secretary-personal assistant to Tallulah, she got shouted out, tantrumed at and taken everywhere. Edie called Tallulah '*die Donner*'.

So this was Home. It was, not surprisingly, a place without boundaries, because Tallulah had never been anywhere where she might have learned about boundaries. Servants were just friends she paid money. She did not know how to look after herself, because who would have taught her that? Everybody was welcome, any time. The home-life of someone working in theatre is peculiar anyway, because your working day starts at The Half, your work energises you into being wide awake into the early hours, and it is a precarious rockface of approval and approbation. You need constant attention and validation because you are creating artifice out of reality. The life of the house careered from long party to long party. In a feature 'The Fun of Open House', Tallulah said she thought guests should only bring essentials. Essentials were 'gramophone records, sandwiches, fruit salads, lime juice, soda-water and gin'. It was all Good Anecdote, Bad Lifestyle. Ethel Barrymore, staying in Tallulah's basement on a London visit, was given a farewell party and missed her sailing date by two days. She gave her reason as 'delayed by English fog'. Days ran into nights, party guests turned into lodgers, last week's party segued into this week's. It must have been more exhausting than running the government.

And all the time, Tallulah was working. Basil Dean offered her the role of Amy in Sidney Howard's *They Knew What They Wanted*. It was a Pulitzer-winner and it had a wonderful, successful Broadway production. The usual media view of Tallulah was this:

> '*Down there on stage she wears clothes that would cost a year's earnings. She moves in expensive apartments at Paris, Deauville, St Jean de Luz. Young men in exquisite evening dress are rivals in love with her. Miss Tallulah Bankhead is on the stage what every woman in the gallery in some degrees wishes to be, the dream fulfilment made manifest.*'

Now here, suddenly, was a play about an ordinary waitress in an Italian restaurant in Napa valley, in a five dollar dress. Tallulah must have known that this was something in which she could be good. Glenn Anders was to replay his role as Tony, her lover, Sam Livesey would be her husband. Directed and produced by Basil Dean, it would open at the St Martin's 18 May 1926. She worked hard, she got into the part and she dropped all her mannerisms. No cartwheels, no underwear. She did great. James Agate wrote 'One had read one's programme with, let it be confessed, something of a sinking heart, for it foreshadowed an actress whose successive incarnations had connoted a fallen angel, a green hat, and a scotch mist. Would this piece be yet another incredible farrago of maidens very far from loath, and epigrammatic noblemen too languid to pursue?' Of course, Schadenfreud-wise, we are all hoping yes! But, 'One's fears were soon allayed. The curtain had not been up five minutes before we knew that Miss Bankhead was to play the part of an ex-waitress in a "spaghetti-joint", or cheap restaurant. Ten minutes later, the actress appeared wearing the cheapest of cotton frocks. At once she set about a piece of sincere emotional acting felt from the heart and controlled by the head, which set up a standard of accomplishment for this clever artist. Miss Bankhead made an instantaneous and great success, and one would seize the occasion to say that to deplore the misdirection of talent is a very different thing from denying its existence. It would be ungenerous not to recognise that her performance in this piece is one of quite unusual merit.'

At last, Tallulah got good reviews for her *acting*. The *Observer*:

> '*She played the part of Amy with a nervous intensity that I hardly suspected her to possess. Her agitation and restless excitement in the first act were superbly done … Miss Bankhead's performance must considerably increase her reputation … '*

and in *The News*:

> '*There were those who were not convinced by her performance in* The Green Hat *and* Scotch Mist *but last night she showed herself a fine artist. Miss Bankhead acted brilliantly.*'

Three points:

a) Tallulah was fucking Glenn Anders. Sexual Chemistry. That *always* gives a play a lift.

b) The plays Tallulah had so far shone in had been *well-written*. I rest my case.

c) Tallulah clearly *had* it. Acting ability. Here was a crossroads. Which path was she going to take?

The one group who hated *They Knew What They Wanted* was The Gallery Girls. They knew what *they* wanted. They wanted *Scotch Mist*. Escape. Romance. Unreality. And not a 'real' Tallulah. A Tallulah in silk underwear and froth, not taking herself seriously and not taking this Acting Lark seriously. And Tallulah missed them.

In 1927, *The Sphere* nominated the ten most remarkable women in the country. In alphabetical order they were: Lady Astor, Tallulah Bankhead, Lady Diana Cooper, the Duchess of Hamilton, Lady Londonderry, Olga Lynn, the Queen, Claire Sheridan, Edith Sitwell, and Mrs Vermet. Apart from the obvious observations of 'hmmm, real rags-to-riches bunch we got here' ... and 'Who is Mrs Vermet?' ... Tallulah was clearly riding the crest of a wave. It was a Top List.

Tallulah returned to her old ways when *They Knew What They Wanted* closed after 108 performances. *The Gold Diggers*, by Avery Hopwood, was a stirring tale of gold-digging girls in gold pyjamas from Molyneux chasing rich men to keep them in the style they would be glad to become accustomed to. The Gallery girls loved it, the critics hated it. Jobyna Howland, the six-foot Dirtmouth from her Algonquin days was in the show, but that was perhaps the only plus.

The next play Tallulah was fortunate to work in was another Avery Hopwood piece, *The Garden Of Eden*. Now, as a title, that is asking for it. And from the moral majority, it got it.

Some critic said 'It is heavily vulgar, as only the German mind can conceive.' (not only pious, but racist as well). Here is another play you will be sorry you missed. Toni Lebrun is a dancer in a low-lit cafe. She refuses to have sex with her female boss and the stinker sacks her. Luckily, she comes across a man who is fascinatingly European, handsome and rich as Croesus. They fall in love, she agrees to marry him. The Family does not approve. It goes all the way to the bride, in wedding dress, appearing at the stop of a flattering flight of stairs ready to pledge her troth. But then, she suddenly contracts *independence*, takes off her wedding dress, revealing herself, for a moment, to her swain's shocked family (and to the *entire* audience of The Lyric Theatre) in fetching cami-knickers, before rushing off into the world to find herself.

The lesbian come-on, the striptease, caused howls, of outrage from the press, and of frenzied delight from The Gallery. The applause after the lesbian scene lasted forever. The Lyric management had to organise a police escort every time Tallulah left the theatre, she was so in danger of being mobbed . Possibly Tallulah's secret awareness that she had substituted gold for trash in her career choice made her cling closely to her Stage Door Jennies. She had them back to her dressing room, even her house. They discovered she wore 'Chypre' perfume and called it out every time she appeared in a scene. Alas, in Cockney, it comes across as 'Sheep, sheep'. Tallulah developed a kind of secret code for the Gallery Girls to keep herself and them amused 'Bye-bye' meant 'beddy-bye', meant 'sex', until her waving nonchalantly as she exited was taken to mean 'I'm off now to have torrid sex'. The play ran for a money-raking 232 performances.

Meanwhile, sex-wise, Tallulah was keeping up the heterosexual side of her palette by sleeping with both Napier Alington and Glenn Anders, and teasing Michael Wardell, who worked for Lord Beaverbrook. Having to miss the first two acts of her First Night, he sent her a diamond brooch. Well, that won't do, will it? She suggested a novel placing for the pinning of the brooch upon his own person. Michael Wardell was one of those relentless boys who can't take no for an answer. Despite the big clue that every time he rang her house his lady love was in the bath ... Paris ... cognito ... he continued to pursue her, even sending in an engineer to put a phone socket in Tallulah's bedroom. Despite

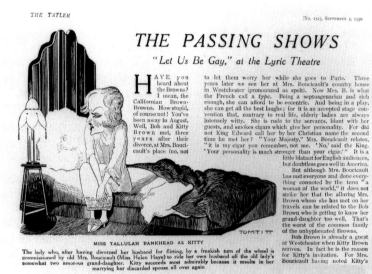

THE PASSING SHOWS
"Let Us Be Gay," at the Lyric Theatre

HAVE you heard about the Browns? I mean, the Californian Brown-Browns. How stupid, of course not! You've been away in August. Well, Bob and Kitty Brown met, three years after their divorce, at Mrs. Boucicault's place (no, not to let them worry her while she goes to Paris. Three years later we see her at Mrs. Boucicault's country house in Westchester (pronounced as spelt). Now Mrs. B. is what the French call a *type*. Being a septuagenarian and rich enough, she can afford to be eccentric. And being in a play, she can get all the best laughs; for it is an accepted stage convention that, contrary to real life, elderly ladies are always intensely witty. She is rude to the servants, blunt with her guests, and smokes cigars which give her personality. For did not King Edward call her by her Christian name the second time he met her? " Your Majesty," Mrs. Boucicault relates, "it is my cigar you remember, not me. 'No,' said the King. 'Your personality is much stronger than your cigar.'" It is a little blatant for English audiences, but doubtless goes well in America.

But although Mrs. Boucicault has met everyone and done everything connoted by the term " a woman of the world," it does not strike her that the alluring Mrs. Brown whom she has met on her travels can be related to the Bob Brown who is getting to know her grand-daughter too well. That's the worst of the common family of the unhyphenated Browns.

Bob Brown is already a guest at Westchester when Kitty Brown arrives. In fact he is the reason for Kitty's invitation. For Mrs. Boucicault having noted Kitty's

TOMTITT

MISS TALLULAH BANKHEAD AS KITTY

The lady who, after having divorced her husband for flirting, by a freakish turn of the wheel is commissioned by old Mrs. Boucicault (Miss Helen Haye) to ride her own husband off the old lady's somewhat two amorous grand-daughter. Kitty succeeds most admirably because it results in her marrying her discarded spouse all over again

A RATHER UNFLATTERING CARTOON OF TALLULAH IN 'THE TATLER',
3 SEPTEMBER 1930

such ingenuity, staying power and him having a black eye patch over the eye he lost in a hunting accident (dashing, or what?) he was soundly ditched. She replaced him with Tony Wilson, grandson to Earl Ribblesdale. He was nineteen.

Sibling rivalry now rears its ugly head. Eugenia, after her second divorce from Morton Hoyt, was living in Paris. She decided to become an actress under the stage name of Sally Hoyt. She had made an indifferent film, the last day of shooting of which she had been temporarily blinded when an arc light exploded beside her. She was never lucky with those eyes. In 1928, eyes now focusing again, they lighted upon The London Stage, on a part in *The Barker*, with Claudette Colbert in the lead. Albert de Couville, the producer, had an idea to exploit the Bankhead connection – '*Another* Bankhead', without checking how close the second Bankhead was to the first. Tallulah did the sisterly support thing, going to the first night in dark glasses dragging along a theatre critic. This foolproof ruse to get her sister on to the first rung of stardom's ladder failed. The critic Alan Parsons merely did a piece on Tallulah visiting the theatre. Critics remarked that 'Miss Hoyt had executed an acceptable can-can'. The show closed early, but not before Eugenia had fallen head over cancan in love with Tony Wilson. The feeling was mutual. They did their fucking at Francis Laking's house, Francis Laking told Tallulah, Tallulah told reporters 'Eugenia's put on some spectacular performances over the years, darling, but none of them have ever been on the goddam stage'. The sisters didn't talk for years. Tallulah consoled herself with *another* Naps fling. Shortly after this, Naps entered a lavender marriage with Lady Mary Ashley-Cooper, which proved happy and enduring.

To show Eugenia, Tony Wilson and Napier Alington that She Just Didn't Care, Tallulah agreed to marry Count Anthony de Bosdari, who she met on a Brighton jaunt. He was short, dark and Italian. Taking the whole thing slowly and sensibly ... he moved in with her three days after their return from Brighton. He gave her a diamond necklace and a rundown on his credentials, which were *massive;* Florentine, connected to Italian royalty, rich, public schoolboy, athlete, good dancer, Tallulah explained him to Daddy:

> *'He has given me the most beautiful diamond necklace and a Rolls Royce for Christmas. He has one already but he is giving me a two-seater Rolls so that I can get some fresh air and exercise at the same time. He also thinks it would be rather chic for me to pick him up at the office. Just a model wife you know. I don't have to give up the stage unless I want to. He's usually right I'm marrying the 22nd of December at the Regent's Office as you are not here to give me away.'*

> *I love you*

> *Tallulah'*

Well, we know it's not going to happen, don't we?

The marriage kept getting postponed. Once, because Tallulah was making a film – *His House In Order* for Ideal Films, again when Tallulah discovered that the dashing Count wasn't *completely* unmarried from his last wife, and then lastly when she worked out that most of his massive credentials were pure hokum.

For the next two years, Tallulah continued to plough a cartwheeling, ad-libbing, cami-knicker-showing furrow, appearing in the forgettable *Mud and Treacle, Her Cardboard Lover, He's Mine, The Lady Of The Camellias* and *Let Us Be Gay.*

Her Cardboard Lover went on a tour. It was a huge box-office success, particularly in Scotland where she was fainted over by Scottish Gallery Girls. She was, for the first time, having difficulty sleeping. She had some plastic surgery on her nose. She was, after all, now in her *mid*-twenties! She continued to get newspaper coverage as a one-woman crusade to spread moral turpitude throughout the realm. Picking up the now forgiven Tony Wilson's brother and brother's friend from Eton for a lunch on the Thames, someone forgot to get permission. The Press took the story and ran with it, until it was whipped up into 'Child Abductor steals children from Public School'. It was rumoured that Eton banned all boys from attending a Tallulah Bankhead play and the occasional 'Child Molestor' heckle penetrated the general adulation.

Then the seraphic Aimee Semple Macpherson, Woman Of God and Businesswoman Of Note came to London, to run gospel sessions to save souls and make money. Beatrice Lillie, to Tallulah 'the funniest woman who ever stood in shoe leather' (and a *terrific* villainess in *Thoroughly Modern Millie!*) decided that the two of them would check Aimee out for sincerity and saintliness. With Leslie Howard, her co-star in *Her Cardboard Lover*, they took Miss Macpherson out for a drink:

> *'We admitted to depravities and excesses – mostly invented – to test her tolerance. She shrugged them off "I don't mind those things so long as you don't hurt anyone else by doing them".'*

Bea Lillie was leaving on The *Leviathan* from Southampton, so they all decided to drive down to see her off. There was terrible fog (the real kind, as well as The Ethel Barrymore Variety) and the journey took forever. The

Press got wind of it, and turned it into Mrs Macpherson's 'All Night Motor Journey Actress Friends Of The Evangelist Reticence Of Her Companions'. It is a *masterly* putting together of thirteen words. It sounds like something *unspeakable* occurred!

Augustus John asked if could do a portrait of her for The Royal Academy Summer Exhibition. She agreed on the condition that she could buy it for £1,000 after the show. The judges described it as 'the greatest portraiture since Gainsborough's Perdita'. Lawrence of Arabia tried to buy it. The Tate wanted it for permanent exhibition. Tallulah kept it until the end of her life.

In late 1928, the Home Secretary assured Radclyffe Hall a place in history when he asked her publisher to discontinue publication of *The Well Of Loneliness*. A *terrible* book, everyone immediately said it was wonderful and supported its continuation. *Things* were being mentioned. Times were changing.

VHF writing in *Theatre Works* got on the case:

> 'No criticism of Tallulah Bankhead's plays is complete without reference to her display of lingerie. Personally, I find her more attractive in a jumper-suit than without one, and I am quite willing to take her underclothes for granted. I am told, however, that these rather feeble attempts at immodesty are for the benefit of the feminine element of the audience. Well, well, girls will be boys.'

Well, don't you just *hate* him? Tallulah defended herself:

> 'I cannot pretend not to enjoy it, that would be hypocritical. I feel greatly complimented by these demonstrations. As far as my deshabille is concerned, when I take off my dress, it is because the play demands it, because it is quite a natural outcome of the plot of the play. There is nothing indelicate about it!'

Offered *The Lady Of The Camellias*, Tallulah took it on to give herself more of a challenge, and get back her 'more-serious-casting' cachet. She wasn't up to it. Her performance was flat, James Agate called it 'an interesting evening in which they will see Tallulah Bankhead make a gallant shot at a play demanding another kind of talent.' Her adoring fans, as Herbert Farjeon put it, preferred her as '*The Lady Of The CamiKnickers*'.

Her last play in London got this review:

> '*Miss Tallulah Bankhead's amazing energy and command of a dozen swiftly variable moods gives some sort of life and lustre even to this stuff. Miss Bankhead hits off the toughness and tenderness, the cheek and charm of the husband-hunters with an easy passage up and down the scale of waywardness. Easy, it seems, but the effort must be enormous. Miss Bankhead never walks through a part; her simulations of caprice are triumphs of conscientiousness. Like all great players she is not so much the public's servant as its drudge, and I never see her act without respecting the diligence as well as the virtuosity of one who gloriously seeks to please.*'

It was time to move on. Paramount Pictures came up with a big money offer for her to make movies.

Pausing only to do *Let Us Be Gay* (with the *old* meaning), written by her old writer friend, Rachel Crothers, she sold her house in Farm Street and took Edie Smith and her latest Crushee, a rich Canadian called Dola Cavendish on the *Aquitania* and left swathed in furs telling the press that 'I've never had a good part yet.' The Gallery Girls gave her a Titanic Send-Off. Here's how she describes the moment:

> '*Professionally I had advanced from comparitive obscurity to international recognition. Fiscally I had receded. I had a letter of credit for a thousand dollars on my arrival; on my departure I had less. I left a lot of debts behind me, a few income tax arrears. But I left a lot of friends behind me too. My eight years in London were the happiest and most exciting in my life.*'

Next stop ... The Movies.

Work, work, work, fuck, fuck, fuck

The author's contribution is the text. If it's good, it doesn't need your help. If it's lacking, there's nothing you can do to aid it. Recognize the fact and learn to live with it — the words and their meaning are not your responsibility. Wisdom lies in doing your job and getting on with it.[12]

Eight years is a long time to be away in theatre. Few theatre-goers and even fewer theatre managements remember Tallulah on the New York stage. Her reputation hangs in some quarters like a recently passed over ghost. But Tallulah arrives back in Diva style, moving into the spiffy Hotel Elysee, handing out magnanimous tips — both of money and on how to behave in England — walks about her hotel suite naked and shocks strait-laced New York with her language, her recent outrageous past and her bare tush. She is letting them know that she is back.

Over the next ten years she will make seven feature films, appear in ten plays and one radio production. Tallulah never gets the best films. She does not play ball with the studios. She is always in work. When she is in well-written parts, she is good. When she isn't, she still obeys the rule as David Mamet cites: 'The rational individual will, when the bell rings, go out there anyway to do the job she said she was going to do. This is called "courage".'

Paramount set up a round of media interviews to get their new star back in the public eye. This was a success. Tallulah, as ever, gave good anecdote. She was informative — if inaccurate — about all aspects of British society, politics, satire. Her originality shone through. She took.

She began shooting *Tarnished Lady* on the Long Island lot of Paramount East. For a now seasoned stage performer, film work was awful. No audience,

TALLULAH BANKHEAD BY AUGUSTUS
JOHN, OIL ON CANVAS, C.1930

everything shot out of sequence, and the interminable waiting around while
the *really important* things like lighting and set were fixed, and the film
overview that actors aren't *that* important drove Tallulah crazy. Tallulah did
what discontented actors do on film sets, she started an affair or two, with
Libby Holman, a torch singer who was supposed to provide research for her
part; and the aviatrix Louisa Carpenter, who became her life-long friend. She
spent weekends at Libby's house at Sands Point, mistook Louisa for a maid
('Run me a bath.' ... 'Run it yourself, lady!') and did the country thing of
going for long walks, although on Tallulah's treks a chauffeured Rolls-Royce

shadowed the trekkers, a gramophone in its back seat playing music by those country hicks Bing Crosby and Ross Columbo.

Tarnished Lady was George Cukor's first solo directing job. George was gay, but he was also in the closet, sneery of out gays, and a rough trade boy. At first he and Tallulah disliked each other. She was out, he was in, she outed him. Eventually, they settled down and became good friends. Neither could do much about the script and plot of the film. She plays a goody-two-shoes type who saves her beloved mother from poverty by going off torch-singing in low dives and then marrying for money. They went on location in Harlem, *just* to film the cabaret scenes, but Tallulah fell in love with the place, visited a lot and got herself photographed dancing cheek to cheek *with a Black Man*! [Now, recall Daddy's views on race from the first chapter?] He sent a cross-father letter to Tallulah. Tallulah, Southern-born girl, was crushed. Her producer, Walter Wanger sent an arse-licking letter to the Congressman saying it was all part of filming. Tallulah continued to visit Harlem, where she made many friends. It was also where she got her cocaine.

Tarnished Lady was released in 1931 with full bells, cannons, whizbangs and a hell of a lot of CAPITAL LETTERS, thus:

> THE PRODUCERS WHO BROUGHT YOU DIETRICH
> BRING YOU ANOTHER WOMAN-THRILL! TALLULAH
> BANKHEAD! SHE ENTHRALLED A NATION! ENGLAND'S
> ADORED BEAUTY ON THE SCREEN! GET WITHIN
> RANGE OF HER RADIANCE! FEEL THE RAPTUROUS
> THRILL OF HER VOICE, HER PERSON!

Marketing & Publicity pushed out the boat. At Preview Night the lobby had a toy-train display and huge photograph portraits of Tallulah wearing *real* sashes. Signs invited: 'THIS GIRL WILL SHOCK YOU – HER PERSONALITY REGISTERS LIKE A THIRD RAIL! PULL THE SASH AND FIND OUT FOR YOURSELF!' Punters brave enough to pull the sashes experienced a mild electric shock. Which was more than the black-tie critical audience experienced. The reviews were awful. Cukor got it in the neck. The audience were bored and laughed in the wrong places. It was felt that Marketing & Publicity's lavish launch idea 'might have been devised for Tallulah by her worst enemy in a particularly cruel moment.'

The best assessment of it came from Tallulah herself in her autobiography, written after the sting had stopped stinging: 'Was it any good? In a word, No! Though it had a fine director, a first-rate writer, and a luminous, er, star, it was a fizzle. Why? For the same reason that though the eggs, the cracker-crumbs and the salt used for a souffle may be top-notch the resultant dish may be rancid. The picture was made by trial and error. What appeared on the screen showed it.'

The ludicrous launch, and the dodgy film got Tallulah's film career off to a shaky start, from which it never really recovered. It is listed in Halliwell's Film Companion for eternity as 'A poor picture that fits the straight grinds best. Heavy production but too ponderous to mean anything'.

Paramount continued to sell her as a rival to Marlene Dietrich with a further outbreak of CAPITALS as in COMING! COMING! TALLULAH THE GLAMOROUS, TALLULAH THE MYSTERIOUS, TALLULAH THE WOMAN, WE GAVE YOU MARLENE DIETRICH NOW WE GIVE YOU TALLULAH BANKHEAD! Tallulah complained that in London, Marlene Dietrich was called the second Tallulah Bankhead. The last shrieky set of CAPITALS was changed to WE GIVE YOU BACK TALLULAH BANKHEAD. The publicity rivalry helped Marlene and Tallulah to develop a healthy rivalry in their personal appreciation of each other. Reviews which said 'Miss Bankhead is not unlike Marlene Dietrich and has the same deep voice' cannot have thrilled either original, while 'She gives a credible impersonation of Marlene Dietrich singing a song' can have thrilled only one.

Tallulah went on to make *My Sin* and *The Cheat* for Paramount. Back to Halliwell for *My Sin*; 'A drunken lawyer helps a woman who has shot her husband. Turgid melodrama which failed to make a screen idol of its star.

Fredric March, Harry Davenport, Scott Kolk, Ann Sutherland, written by Owen David & Adelaide Heilbron from the story by Frederick Jackson. Directed for Paramount by Paramount.' 'Fair returns will be top.'

Richard Watts Jr, critic, said 'At least they have photographed the eminent Miss Bankhead properly in *My Sin*. It remains, nevertheless, another mean trick to play on a fine actress and brilliant personage who is waiting for a part worthy of her.' Tallulah describes herself in this film as 'a notorious hussy loose in the Canal Zone, up to some erotic nonsense in a cabaret.' It was 'flubdub'. I am, hereafter, a lifelong fan of the term 'flubdub'.

In both films, she played po-faced temptresses with a *past* who always seemed to have cabaret-singing as their only career choice. They were always the human tennis ball being whacked between two men. She wore outfits best suited for late-night work and she always looked physically ill-at-ease. Her reviews were not good. Paramount decided to play a long game, however, raised her salary from $5,000 to $6,000 a week and kept her on contract, hoping that eventually she would blossom filmically. The image-makers were a little confused as to how to market her because they had got her down as European. But she did not 'smoulder' like, say, Pola Negri, or mutter exotically like Garbo and Dietrich. It never occurred to them to sell her as *herself*.

They sent her out on a date with Gary Cooper to see *This Year Of Grace*, with Noel Coward and Beatrice Lillie. There were high expectations. Tallulah fancied Cooper from afar and, as she said in her girlish way, had 'not experienced a goddam good penetration' since getting back. However, Cooper, on his knees from consecutive hot affairs with 'Mexican Spitfire' Lupe Velez, and 'Social Mushroom' Countess Dorothy de Frasco, was terrified of 'Shag 'Em' Bankhead. Cooper said not one word all evening. Tallulah never stopped to draw breath. Something went well however, as they had a brief fling, its gentle romantic nature somewhat besmirched by Tallulah's open bragging about Cooper's 'two-hander-trouser-snake'.

About this time, Tallulah was trying to find a good secretarial assistant. She was foolish enough to mention it to my old favourite, Aunt Marie. Aunt Marie applied for the post, at a salary of $5,000 a year. 'This is a hint, not an application. I will say that my five years experience in a newspaper office has made of me a first rate "publicity man"; my social experience has civilised me; and my love for you would warrant me in becoming a shock absorber between you and the clamorous public.' Now, I'd have employed her like a shot, but Tallulah was gentle without ever being affirmative. She persuaded her that she would serve posterity better by concentrating on her writing career.

Paramount sent Tallulah to Hollywood. She persuaded Audry and Kenneth Carten, on a three-week holiday to visit her, to take the four and a half day train ride to Hollywood with her. They read, ate, drank, laughed and slept their way across the continent. Douglas Fairbanks Jr and his newish wife, Joan Crawford, were also on the train. Crawford invited the Tallulah party to dinner. Fairbanks remembers the evening beginning with Tallulah sticking her head round the door with 'I've already fucked your husband, darling. Soon it'll be your turn.' Tallulah, as the dinner invitation was advertised as a strictly informal do, turned up in slacks, only to find Joan rigged out as if she was going to the opera. Crawford remembers Tallulah as 'very sweet, but she frightened the bejesus out of me!' They all settled down to a game of 'Truth', which broke up when Crawford decided not to answer the question 'Have you ever been unfaithful to your husband?' She objected on the grounds that 'since none of you are married, I don't think it proper to discuss the subject.'

Tallulah decided to rent film star Bill Haines' mansion on North Stanley Avenue because, as she told the real-estate agent, she 'simply *had* to sleep in the room where Bill Haines got it together with that *divine* Clark Gable'. Known as 'Lavender Lips', Louis B. Mayer had called him 'lip-lazy' on his voice test. Bill Haines remarked that he had never had any complaints before. Tallulah hired three black servants and treated them as friends, particularly in front of her sometime racist friends, bought two Rolls Royces because 'Cars are like men ... It's much better to have a couple on standby in case one breaks down.' She wore slacks, she went walking, she worked on her tan.

Her first film in Hollywood was *Thunder Below*. Stand back, here come the Capitals again;

ONE WOMAN DESIRED, DESIRING – IN A VILLAGE OF LONELY MEN BELOW THE EQUATOR, WHERE CIVILISATION'S BARRIERS SWIFTLY BURN AWAY

Tallulah played another female tennis-ball between a husband and his best friend. It had Charles Bickford as rugged husband, Paul Lukas as tastier friend. *Variety* described it as 'Star as weak as story ... dull and uneventful.' Yes, it was flubdub. Tallulah was beginning to be seen as box-office poison. The bright spot in this piece of work was director Paul Wallace, who Tallulah described as 'a divine man. Don't wince at my adjective. It hasn't intruded often in this saga'. Having once been a mortician's assistant, he took her for a picnic in a mortuary. *Just* Tallulah's kind of Pig Race.

For a heart-stopping moment, it seemed as though Tallulah would take over from Marlene Deitrich in *Blonde Venus*, when the head of Paramount, B. P. Schulberg, took exception to one scene. Poor Marlene/Tallulah has to take to prostitution to pay for her sick husband's radium treatment – there are no child-care arrangements on that sort of job – and she has to take the kid with her and hide him under the table while she touts for customers. Von Sternberg, the director, walked off set, taking his protegee, Marlene with him. Tallulah, who had 'always wanted to get into Marlene's pants' took over. Hearing that Miss Dietrich sprinkled gold dust in her hair – head *and* pubic – Tallulah sprinkled *her* hair with gold dust and said 'Guess where *I've* just been?' Schulberg and Sternberg settled their differences, Marlene came back and Tallulah was offered ...

Make Me A Star: a grocery clerk goes to Hollywood and becomes a film star. 'Packed with laughs which offsets the longish running time'. Tallulah's name was removed from the credits. Well, *we're* not going to bother with *that* then, are we?

Tallulah, who was hating movie work, was very keen to go back on stage. A writ served for $15,000 in back taxes decided her. It was back to movies with *The Devil and The Deep*, a turgid melodrama in which a submarine commander went mad with jealousy over his faithless wife. The starry cast included Charles Laughton, Gary Cooper, Cary Grant, Paul Porcasi. *Variety* called it 'Of femme interest despite the lukewarm performance of Tallulah Bankhead ... a fair commercial release'. Charles Laughton stole all the notices. The film ends with husband, lover and wife (in sequins and stilettos, *de rigeur* dress for submarines) in a life or death tussle. Laughton opened all the hatches, despite being captain and *knowing* that was not submarine procedure. Cooper the lover and Bankhead the wife escaped death by drowning by climbing a rope to the surface. The last lines were, Wife: 'I want never to have been born', Lover: 'There's magic out there. Do you want to kill it?'

Well, *I'm* sorry I missed it. The film was her most successful so far. In it, they had made her look more like a second Garbo than a second Dietrich. She was short of money. She asked for a rise. She was turned down. She had a tantrum. She threatened to leave Hollyood 'Forever!' to go back and help out her poor family in Alabama (What? Who?). Paramount reached an elegant compromise by sending her on loan to MGM.

Did this lead to better film roles for her? MGM put her in *Faithless*. You decide: 'A spoiled rich girl and her beau both descend to working class level and almost further. Would-be sensational drama ruined by censorship and miscasting.' With Robert Montgomery, Hugh Herbert, Maurice Murphy, Louise Closser Hale, Lawrence Grant, Henry Kolker, it was written by Carey Wilson from the novel *Tinfoil* by Mildred Cram and directed by Harry Beaumont and produced by Oliver T. March. 'They pile the suffering on so thick that any but the most naive theatre-goers are going to revolt and scoff.'

1932 was the year the Hays office came up with The Motion Picture Code, which outlawed filming acts of indecency like kissing with your mouth open, hairy chests, and using beds as anything but places to sleep, read and drink cocoa. Its inception coincided, unfortunately, with a ripe and salty, no-holds-barred interview Tallulah gave to Gladys Hall for Motion Picture Magazine on the subject of 'I Want A Man'. Hays immediately demanded that Tallulah be dropped by MGM on a severance pay of absolutely-not-one-red-cent. Tallulah did a patch-up interview in which her sincere remorse shines like a red brothel lamp. 'I have followed Mr Hay's advice and have taken up a completely sexless, nun-like, legs-crossed existence.' She declared that the man she was living with 'Certainly isn't sleeping in *my* bed', and pointed out a beautiful young actor called Anderson Lawlor who was waving to a photographer through Tallulah's bedroom window as 'Oh him? He's just the new stud I've engaged until someone better comes along!' Hays responded by insisting on a change of ending for *Faithless*. Despite this, the critics on the whole, liked it. Tallulah demanded another pay rise. Louis B. Mayer called her into his office and with great generosity offered her Jean Harlow's part in *Red Dust*. Tallulah refused on the grounds of actress solidarity. Mayer was firing Harlow because her husband had got bad publicity for the company on account of inconsiderately committing suicide and in the ensuing spat Mayer brought up Tallulah's sexual adventures, and Tallulah brought up the fact that the adventures were with MGM luminaries Jobyna Howland, Barbara Stanwyk, Joan Crawford, and what was the phone number of the press? ...

Now she really *was* going back to The Stage. As she said in her autobiography:

> '*Remember '32? It was the year in which Florenz Ziegfeld, Minnie Maddern and John Philip Sousa died, that the bonus army marched on Washington, that Lindbergh's baby was kidnapped, that Amelia Earhart flew the Atlantic, that Jimmy Walker resigned as mayor of New York, that a man named Hitler ran second to Hindenberg in the German elections. It was also the year we hit the bottom of the depression. Banks were folding up like concertinas. Paramount had similiar symptoms.*'

She threw a stonking good farewell party and took the train for New York. She had made $250,000. With relief she recounts 'It would be twelve years before I'd face a motion picture camera again.'

'THE BLACK WIDOW' IN BATMAN. TALLULAH OFTEN CLAIMED THAT SHE WAS THE INVENTOR OF CAMP ... SHE HAD NO PROBLEMS WITH THE ROLE

Barged down the Nile and sank

Tallulah Bankhead returned to New York in 1933 with a strong need to have more *control* over the work she did. So she became her own producer, setting up a production of *Forsaking All Others*, a script written by E. B. Roberts and Frank Cavett, a cameraman on *The Devil And The Deep*. She and the ever-loyal Edie Smith booked into *The* Hotel – The Gotham – and she financed the production herself, keeping that fact from the media. She engaged Fred Keating, a magician in his first straight-acting role, as her leading man, Ilka Chase as her love-rival and Anderson Lawlor as second male lead. Don Oenslanger was set designer, Hattie Carnegie did costumes and Harry Wagstaffe Gribble was director. It had, not surprisingly, an extremely ramshackle and rough ride pre-preview, opening in Boston and then on to Washington. Five hundred Gallery Girls turned up in Boston, listening only to Tallulah's lines, drowning out other actors, shying missiles at Fred Keating's character and booing Ilka Chase's love-rival. In Washington, the theatre management – scared shitless – ruled that Gallery Girls would not be admitted, this was The Capital, *Politicians* would be in the audience. Our Actress-Manager pulled rank and threatened not to go on. The decision was overruled and Congressman Daddy, as ladies' knickers rained down from the upper reaches of the theatre, finally must have realised his little girl was a Dyke. Tallulah spent the evening after the show encouraging her father to chat up Jean Dalrymple, one of the cast. It may have been an attempt to sidetrack questions about her sexuality, it may have been a piece of Freudian loose-ticketry. Who knows? I think Daddy might, about this stage, have started averring that Tallulah was 'a career girl' (Parentspeak for 'I don't want to *think* about it'). The production moved into New York on a stomach-churning swathe of sacking. The director was replaced, as was Tallulah's agent. Jean Dalrymple, who criticised the Gallery Girls' behaviour was threatened but kept on. Daddy's Friend. The play ran for 14 weeks but was not a success. Tallulah lost $40,000 of her own money (could have *told* her!), which she recovered when she sold the screen rights to MGM. It was rewritten by Joseph Mankiewiz and was a big hit for Crawford and Gable. Through it she also met a new 'caddie' – John Hay Whitney.

These caddies were good-looking and useful types who were any sexuality and gender, but who lived with Tallulah and performed deeply-necessary tasks, such as lighting her cigarettes, keeping her company and looking after the running of the Tallulah Road Show. Sometimes she slept with them, sometimes not. Sometimes they were loyal, honest and stayed forever-friends. Sometimes they weren't and didn't. They seem to me a great invention that has gone sadly out of fashion. They were also fake family.

With the MGM money from *Forsaking All Others* Tallulah decided to put on *Jezebel*. She took a little holiday first, staying at The Garden Of Allah (which the afore-mentioned Nazimova had turned into a money-spinning celebrity getaway) where she kept company with the composer Vincent Youmans (*Tea For Two, I Want To Be Happy, More Than You Know, Rise'n'Shine,Time On My Hands* and *Hallelujah*) – she got him into bed once – and Johnny Weismuller, of *Tarzan* fame, who she seduced by jumping into Nazimova's pool, screaming, so he dived in and pulled her out naked, making her as she said, 'a very satisfied Jane'.

Five days into rehearsals for *Jezebel* she got ill. She had crippling abdominal pains and was in hospital for nine weeks, while the press reported it as kidney stones, colic, pregnancy and even as 'Bankhead wants to get out of *Jezebel*, and has resorted to the ruse of the invalid.' She was released and ordered to rest completely, which she did for twenty-four hours, then went back to rehearsals. She was living on cigarettes, codeine and bourbon. No food. She collapsed again and was rushed back into hospital. For those with an interest in medicine, here is Doctor Tallulah Bankhead MD's clinical self-diagnosis:

> '*I was on the operating table for five hours.What they found in my abdominal cavities and adjacent areas was hair-raising.There was a technical name for the contortions of my innards, but I can't remember it. My trunk lines were matted,*

meshed and fouled up. To climax my woe, I developed as pretty a set of chilblains as you'll ever lay eyes on. To this day I wince at the sight of an icebag. I was hospitalised for fifteen weeks.'

Actually, she had gonorrhea. She had a bowel obstruction removed and an enormous hysterectomy. She almost died. Her weight dropped to 73 pounds. She was discharged, hired a private nurse, and went very quiet. There was now no possibility of ever having children. She was thirty. She saw only her nurse, Anderson Lawlor and Edie Smith. She was depressed. Anderson and Edie became afraid that she was going mad and they would have to section her. The madness proved to be a mixture of being denied codeine on the one hand, and ingesting smuggled cocaine and bourbon on the other. Miriam Hopkins opened in her part in *Jezebel*; critical opinion closed the show in four weeks. 'Had I been it it, it might have lasted *five* ...' said The Good Patient. Over Christmas she convalesced in Jasper, and then decided to go to England to cheer herself up. She was described in the press as 'quieter and more serious than in days gone by'. She banged about England partying and doing impersonations for various charities. She saw her friends and her touch-stone people, the Cartens. She got better. 'I shook off the melancholia which had sporadically gripped me in New York and Hollywood, and had a rip-roaring good time.' She was a brave woman, brave, brave, brave.

She returned to New York – in a blue Schiaperelli dress, carrying two Pekinese dogs, Sally and Ann – to do *Dark Victory*. This was a play about a young woman who gives up being bright, young and outrageous when she discovers she has cancer of the brain. Robert Benchley called it 'Camille without the coughing'. It was touted as a great stage vehicle for her, and if not for stage, then a great screen vehicle. Tallulah had views: 'I thought otherwise. Why? I had read it. I had read it in at least six of its variations.' She did the worst thing you can do, however, she did not follow her first instinct to run like a stag. She was won over by the producer, Jock Anderson. The reviews for the play were bad. The stage vehicle crawled along for 51 performances. Tallulah got ill again. This cost her the role in the screen version. Like *Jezebel*, the part went to Bette Davis, who won a second Oscar.

Then – what goes round goes round ... She was offered *Rain*. She was still miffed with Maugham, she thought the public would compare her unfavourably to Jeanne Engels in the earlier, smash-hit production, and, once again, she did not obey her first instinct. The producer Sam Harris said he was mounting it at the Music Box Theater which had never had a single flop. Tallulah was swayed and proved that there was a first time for eveything.

Next came *Something Gay*, which opened 29 April 1935 at The Morosco Theater: 'as misleading a title as ever was hung on two hours of plot and dialogue.' Most people are united in the opinion that this was the worst pile of flubdub (with *stiff* competition) that Tallulah had ever been in. Despite a good director, Tommy Mitchell and the stalwart Walter Pidgeon as co-star, nobody could breathe life into the piece. 'It was a goddamn entombment', admitted Tallulah. It shuddered to a halt after nine weeks, 'unwept save by Adelaide Heilborn who wrote it, and by the brothers Shubert who produced it.'

Tallulah was getting anxious. She could not get a hit. She had now been out of work for nearly a year. Then she got a bit lucky. George Kelly was a writer with a popular and critical record. He had had hits with plays *The Torchbearers, The Show-Off, Daisy Mame, Behold The Bridegroom* and a Pultizer Prize for *Craig's Wife*. It tried out in San Francisco and Los Angeles. He had a new play, *Reflected Glory*. It was about an actress who has to choose between a marriage and a successful stage career. She chose the stage. George Kelly makes this seem the right decision. Early feminism. Tallulah played the actress. It did well on the West Coast and Tallulah began to feel hopeful. Then, on 21 September 1936 it came into New York, to the Morosco Theater. The critics decided that it was the requisite duff play from a fine writer, and slammed it. Tallulah remembers: 'Had it been by a lesser playwright, I think they would have cheered it. Kelly was the victim of his own high standards.'

In June of 1936, the speaker of The House Of Representatives had died unexpectedly, and Congressman Will Bankhead had become his successor, making Daddy a Major Cheese. He introduced the Farm Tenancy Bill, enabling farmers in dire straits to get government loans, and the Relief Deficiency Bill. America's Poor were going through lean times after the Wall

Street Crash. He attended *Reflected Glory* in Washinton and presented his daughter with a lucky rabbit's foot, which she kept forever.

David O. Selznick had read Margaret Mitchell's *Gone With The Wind* and had bought the film rights. He had started his own film company, but he needed more backing. Luckily, his father-in-law was Louis B. Mayer and for the one and a quarter-million Mayer investment, Selznick had to take MGM's Clark Gable to play Rhett Butler. Norma Shearer was to play Scarlett O'Hara, then changed her mind, and for the next two years the script was delivered to every castable actress (and several non-castable ones too) in the Hollywood Hills. Pencilled in were Bette Davis, Joan Crawford, Claudette Colbert, Carole Lombard, Katherine Hepburn, Margaret Sullavan, Olivia de Havilland and many, many producers' and directors' mistresses. Olivia de Havilland was given the *good girl* part Melanie and Leslie Howard became upright but wussy Ashley Wilkes. John Hay Whitney put Tallulah's name forward. Selznick went to see *Reflected Glory*. He immediately wired Father-in-Law WE'VE GOT SCARLETT. Father-In-Law asked who that might be – what goes round goes round – (Remember Tallulah's departure from MGM?) Son-in-Law was told to 'look a little further'.

'I knew I could play the pants off Scarlett. I looked upon myself as a symbol of the South, the fine flower of its darkest hours. Temple bells rang in my head, and I whiffed the scent of the magnolias,' Tallulah wrote 'For months I was leading in the Scarlett Derby whilst Selznick and his aides kept looking in treetops, under bridges, in the Social Register, and on the lists of parolees from reformatories. But my bones told me I wouldn't get the part ...'

Aunt Marie organised the sending of many, many letters to Selznick. Alabama wanted Scarlett to be played by a native-borne Southern. It was a publicity jamboree. The favourite could not win. It had to be an outsider, a 23-1 shot. Enter Vivien Leigh ...

Cukor was up to direct. Suddenly he was replaced with Victor Fleming. There was a fuck-link – Cukor to Bill Haines, and Bill Haines to Clark Gable. Rhett Butler simply could *not* be outed as a faggot. Tallulah could

TALLULAH MARRIED JOHN
EMERY ON 31 AUGUST 1937
AND DIVORCED, CITING MENTAL
CRUELTY, FOUR YEARS LATER.
WHO WAS MENTALLY CRUEL
TO WHO IS NOT DOCUMENTED

therefore not be trusted to be a tight-lipped goodie-goodie playing Scarlett.
So Vivien Leigh got into the stays and the white frock. Hattie Carmichael
laced her up. And Tallulah, with all the other hopefuls, retired hurt. The rest
is Movie History. Well, we've all seen *Gone With The Wind*. It's great. But
Tallulah as Scarlett? Now *that* I would like to have seen.

Now ... Tallulah's marriage. Her only marriage. Why? Let's think. She is now
thirty-five. Her sister Eugenia is now contemplating her *seventh* marriage, her
last six, three of which were to Morton Hoyt, have not lasted. Daddy, I am
sure, wants grandchildren, such a triumph as he had made of raising *his*
children. Like the character she played in *Reflected Glory*, Theatre and Screen
must have seemed like a bit of a tough row to hoe ... and anyway, sometimes,
you just make a mistake!

John Emery (the prospective husband) was appearing as Lord Peter Wimsey in *Busman's Honeymoon*, by Dorthy L. Sayers. Sayers' aristocratic detective hero is *so* clever and, once he and Harriet Vane fall in love, get married, and go on honeymoon, he gets *very sexy*. I think this is what happened to Tallulah – she thought she was marrying Lord Peter Wimsey! It only needed an unexpected piece of actor's bravery (a prop curtain caught fire, and Emery put it out with his *bare hands*), for Tallulah to fall hook, line and ...

Ever the sensible woman, she asked advice from her close, serious friends. 'Everybody should be married once', said Estelle Winwood, and 'I've always wanted a trip to Reno', said Edie Smith. He seemed a good listener, thought his bride. They were married at Daddy's house on 31 August 1937 ... she was granted a divorce, on the grounds of mental cruelty, on June 13 1941. Who was mentally cruel to who isn't detailed. Emery said of the marriage 'It was like the rise, decline, and fall of The Roman Empire.'

The actual wedding whizzed by in a haze of bad behaviour and bourbon. On the plane flight to Daddy's house she tried to have sex with her husband in front of the pilot and other passengers. The pilot intervened, so she showed *him* she wasn't wearing underwear by flinging up her skirt, then begged for cunnilingus while hanging from the luggage straps. At the marriage service, the 103rd Psalm was read. Tallulah cried. The Honeymoon was quieter, then they moved into The Gotham because Tallulah was starring in *Antony and Cleopatra* ('I've worked with plenty of snakes in my time'), and she decided John Emery should be in it too. They would be the new Lunts. What could go wrong?

Well, everything. On the very busy set, somewhat over-sphinxed, were an array of contrasting acting styles, according to Aunt Marie too much 'Egyptian politics' and Tallulah, among many awful reviews, got the classic 'Tallulah barged down the Nile last night as Cleopatra – and sank.' The happy couple retired to their hotel suite to lick their wounds. John had been reviewed quite favourably, but he suggested they called room service for some cyanide. They partied. John was a heavy, constant drinker. Once married to Tallulah, the drinking became heavier, more constant. John's latest movie *The Road Back* received awful reviews. Tallulah had to be circumspect about the plays she took on, because she was now The Speaker's Daughter. Money was running out. Edie Smith wrote to Aunt Marie 'just between you and me, I don't know how much longer we can hold out.'

The happy couple appeared in Maugham's *The Circle*, then toured in a Zoe Akins play, *I Am Different*. The play was an old-fashioned comedy, but the marriage by now was no comedy at all, with Tallulah depressed and drinking, and John carrying her on and off trains. Tallulah was performing mechanically, chatting in the wings and then coming on and corpsing. Within two years they were openly badmouthing each other's sexual performances. John said she 'talked a good lay' and complained of being married to Tallulah *and* all her caddies. Tallulah thought he was no fun because he didn't like her picking up men on the street. They were now staying at The Elysee, where the guests complained of the noise, drinking, foul language and excess. 'About three in the morning, Tallulah and the gang were, I suspect, throwing safes at each other. It certainly sounded that way.'

Three years in, and they both started tacitly seeing other people, Tallulah a young English actor, Colin Keith-Johnson, and Emery, Tamara Geva, a ballerina who had defected from Russia in the mid-twenties to join Diaghilev. After four years of drinking and hell the marriage folded. They eventually became friends. Tallulah, with customary generosity, absolved him of blame: 'My interests and enthusiasms are too random for sustained devotion, if you know what I mean ... Other actor pairs have loved and married and endured. Witness the Lunts, Vivien Leigh and Laurence Olivier. Witness John Emery and Tamara Geva. Miss Geva is John's wife and has been these past ten years. She's a damned good actress too. After twenty years of unbridled freedom, of acting on whim, I couldn't discipline myself to the degree necessary for a satisfactory union. I had roamed the range too long to be haltered ... '

Our heroine is now thirty-four, somewhat tossed and buffeted by nearly twenty years in the fast lane. With one failed heterosexual union behind her and before her, a developing history of chronic illness, Does she plump for a mature and sensible life-style involving an exercise regime, yoga, organic vegetables, early nights and just the one glass of red wine with dinner? Does she find the love of a good woman, embrace faithfulness and settle down?

Read on.

TALLULAH (LEFT) WITH EUGINIA RAWLS IN 'THE LITTLE FOXES'

What art!

> *'When, many years hence,*
> *people of the future gaze on this place*
> *they will say,*
> *Aaah,*
> *Aaah ... this is to do with this*
> *and this is to do with this.*
> *How very interesting Art is!'*[13]

If this were a fictitious tale of a motherless child who becomes an actress, travels to London to find fame and fortune, returns home, fails in the movies, fails in her marriage, we would all now be desperate for her to have *some* good luck, wouldn't we, gentle Reader? Well, Life imitates Art. At *last* Tallulah got a part she could run with. At *last* she gets both a critical and popular success! She is virtually drinking herself to death when Lillian Hellman offered her the part of Regina Giddens in *The Little Foxes*. Tallulah immediately recognised Regina as a part to die for.

> *'Up to this time most of my roles had been on the light and larkish side. Though generally playing a woman who didn't give a fig for the commandments, I usually had redeeming qualities – gaiety, a racy and rowdy attitude towards life. Regina permitted no such compromises. She was soulless and sadistic, an unmitigated murderess. For profit she would have slit her mother's throat, but not before so staging the crime that the guilt would be pinned on another.'*

The piece was a fiercely anti-Capitalist piece, which, because of the political colour of the time, became perceived as a fiercely Communist work of Art. Many people thought Tallulah had taken on the play without understanding its politics. Many people underestimated Tallulah. Herman Shumlin was both producer and director and he started rehearsals with trepidation. He wanted Tallulah to play *Regina*, not another Tallulah-flapper-performance. She responded to him well. She liked Eugenia Rawls, the understudy for Florence Williams, who played Regina's beleagured daughter. She liked Richard Maney, the publicity agent (he would later ghost her autobiography). So she had playmates. She had fun with a po-faced, Bible-thumping reporter who wanted to do a 'Most Shameful Woman In America Story' on Tallulah, behaving like a pussy-cat during the interview, then as the woman left through a crowded lobby, called out 'Thank you for the most *marvellous* interview, darling, you're quite the politest lesbian I've ever met!' She had a victorious tussle with Patience Collinge, who played Birdie Hubbard, over the precise level of the heating in the theatre.

The play previewed in Baltimore on 30 January 1939. Tallulah had bronchitis. The Bankhead family turned out in force, with Lillian Hellman and her lover Dashiel Hammett. Feeling like death from the bronchitis, she fell back into her old groove of playing to her Gallery Girls and over-acting. Critics opined that she was 'confusing Regina with Lady Macbeth'. The aftershow party was memorable for a satisfactory spat between Tallulah and Hammett. Tallulah felt Hammett was treating the waiters like slaves. Hammett felt Talluah was treating them like studs. Both views may well have held some germs of truth. The play stumbled into the 41st Street National Theater on 15 February 1939, and once the bronchitis cleared up, and also the bourbon and cigarette cure which she had self-prescribed to clear up the bronchitis worked its homeopathic magic, Tallulah suddenly found her character and became very, very good. The critics realised she was playing the role of her life:

> '*As the vulpine lady, Miss Bankhead is a fox out of hell, sultry, cunning and vicious. Her performance suggests a combination of trade-marked Southern charm, and the spirit of The Borgias to breed a carbolic acid sugarfoot. She is Cindy Lou and Madame Dracula, honeysuckle and deadly nightshade, all done in a magnetic performance that is brilliantly sustained and fascinating.*'

The Little Foxes was nominated for the Drama Critic Circle's Award and

Tallulah herself won the Variety Citation for Best Actress. The show did a benefit night for the Abraham Lincoln Brigade, for wounded survivors of the Spanish Civil War. When Congressman Martin Dies threatened the WPA Federal Theater Project because it 'employs members of the Communist Party and Communist Sympathisers' (we're in that jolly old McCarthy era, folks!) Tallulah fought back, becoming 'The Joan Of Arc' of the WPA. She gave a belter of a speech to The Senate, for which she received a standing ovation, but some months later Congress terminated the Federal Theater Project. The House Appropriations Committee accused Actors Equity of bringing down its demise because they were riddled with communists and named Equity's representative Edith Van Cleve, as having communist sympathies. Edith was a friend of Tallulah's. Tallulah went to the press to establish Edith's non-communist credentials. Despite Tallulah being fiercely anti-communist, a friend is a friend.

By now of course, Britain and the Allied Forces were at war with Germany. When Russia invaded Finland, hundreds of thousands of refugees needed international aid. Tallulah learned about this from ex-President Hoover over an Algonquin lunch attended by Helen Hayes, Gertrude Lawrence, Lee Shubert and Katherine Hepburn. Tallulah agreed on Lillian Hellman and Herman Shumlin's behalf to do a fund-raising performance of *Little Foxes*. Wrong move. Hellman saw quite clearly that if America sided with Finland, the chances of it drawing America into the war were strong. She and Shumlin issued a statement. The benefit did not take place. It was the beginning of a run of vibrant set-tos the management would have with its star over the run of the play. In a week dedicated to helping Finland, snappily called *Finland Week*, Tallulah gave a statement 'Mr Shumlin did not hesitate when donating his time, mental activity and money to the Loyalist Causes in China and Spain. So why not Finland? Human suffering has nothing to do with creed, race, or goddam politics.' Oh yes it does, Tallulah.

After playing for over 400 performances in New York, *The Little Foxes* embarked on an immensely successful spring tour to Washington, Detroit, Boston and Chicago. It broke box-office records everywhere. In Chicago she gave a party for Noel Coward, Clifton Webb and Katherine Hepburn, whom she called 'her three Queens'. In Toronto, a party of kilted soldiers came backstage to see her ('I *love* men in frocks!') She used her Southern Big Cheese influence to get citizenship for a young director called Otto Preminger. She pulled strings, wrote letters and chatted up Daddy's friends into accelerating his acceptance into American life.

While the others in the production rested for summer, Tallulah improved upon the shining hour by taking the lead in *The Second Mrs Tanqueray* and having an affair with Colin Keith-Johnston. She persuaded Eugenia Rawls and Stephen Cole, a caddie, to join the production, because she was lonely. The backstage squabbles achieved a spectacular notoriety in a field of big competition but when it opened at The Maplewood Playhouse, New Jersey, critics said 'Tallulah Bankhead brings a certain majesty that even a playwright could not hope to create with mere words.'

It was a European fad for actresses to keep exotic pets. Josephine Baker had both a pig and a leopard, who wore diamond collars and went for walks down the Champs-Elysees (how come the leopard didn't eat the pig, or vice-versa?), and Mistinguett had thrilled New York society with an ape, which masturbated on cue (the *training!*) Not to be left out, Tallulah bought a marmoset (oh, Tallulah, remember your co-star in *Conchita*), but it bit her as she sung 'Bye Bye Blackbird' to it. So she exchanged it for a rather tired lion cub. The poor thing was taken for walks and then tied up in the dressing-room until it was brought on for curtain calls. He was called Winston Churchill and when asked what would happen when he got bigger, Tallulah said 'I'll ask for a bigger dressing-room.' Winston soon fell out with Tallulah ... returned to zoo work.

The Little Foxes returned for a further tour (why kill the goose that laid the golden egg?). This would have been a fine, easy tour, but Will Bankhead fell ill and was rushed to hospital. Knowing he was dying, Tallulah went on, getting through lines like 'Grief makes some people laugh and some people cry'; 'You've had a bad shock today, I know that'; and 'you loved Papa, but you expected this to come some day. You know how sick he was'.

It must have been unbearable. Two hours later, Daddy died. Tallulah was on the train heading for Washington. Her father was pronounced dead at 1.35a.m. There was a State funeral, attended by The President. Will was taken to Jasper and buried in the family plot. Tallulah missed the Jasper burial. She was an actress. She had gone back to her play. Some months later she went to visit his grave. Interred next to his parents, whose epitaph read 'Here lies a man who inaugurated Federal Aid for Highways', his headstone read, slightly more poetically 'Good night, Sweet Prince, and Flights of Angels Sing Thee To Thy Rest'.

In November, a month after her father died, Napier Alington (Naps), now a fighter pilot in the Royal Air Force, was killed in action in the Battle Of Britain.

The role of Regina went, in the movie version, to Bette Davis. Again.

It was another tough year. She got divorced the following year. She had lost a husband, a father and a long-lost love and friend. She was now officially an orphan. She was now on the back row of the family photograph. Her blood family, in words by her cousin Marion, saw her thus: 'The family saw her a couple of times a year, maybe. She was like a buzz-saw. She was on *all* the time. She *never* got off the stage with anybody. Really, she wore you out, she never stopped.' Her family weren't actors. They didn't know that, in tough times, being *on* feels the safest place to be.

Daddy's death was never mentioned in any of her subsequent interviews. It was clearly a no-go area. It couldn't be laughed off with a smart remark.

Tallulah, the war now into its middle period, became a principal force in the Committee To Defend America by Aiding the Allies. She zipped up and down the country, attending rallies and performing belting patriotic speeches. And more, as the allied troops retreated from the Dunkirk beaches, Tallulah made the ultimate sacrifice: after drinking three hefty cocktails of champagne, gin and brandy with lemon juice to give it a kick, (I'm impressed) she foreswore booze until the Allies could see Hitler off (even more impressed).

Tallulah kept to her word, despite the occasional 'medicinal' tot, (she was *very* prone to sudden colds and stomach upsets at that time!) she lived a pure life, with only cocaine and cigarettes to console her.

The Little Foxes continued to play all over the country. When the company rested, Tallulah found time to appear in a revival of *Her Cardboard Lover*, a Clifford Odets play, *Clash by Night* and to record *Little Foxes*, *The Talley Method* and *Suspicion* for CBS radio. *Clash By Night* was produced by Billy Rose, remembered by us today fondly as the James Caan–acted character in *Funny Lady*, Barbra Streisand's second film about Fanny Brice. Tallulah *hated* Rose. He talked to his cast through a megaphone and on the Theatre front the sign read 'Billy Rose Presents Tallulah Bankhead'. Tallulah said if it did, she would add, 'Billy Rose Present Tallulah Bankhead Absent!'. She called him a goddamm bully, and Billy Rose said 'I once directed an angry herd of buffalo (what play was *that?*) and I once shot an actor out of a cannon fifty feet into the air into the arms of an adagio dancer, but neither of these events was as tough as saying good morning to Tallulah Bankhead.' It was a very unhappy production. Tallulah got pneumonia during the try-outs and was on the critical list for two days but, Doctor Theatre, she brought the play into New York. The critics were unenthusiastic and the play closed after 49 performances.

Some of her behaviour was bizarre. When local journalist Gretchen Gray came to interview her in Jasper, Tallulah disappeared 'to make herself respectable', and got completely naked and ran into the garden. She met Emery when her tour and his of *Skylark* crossed in St Louis. They 'spent the night in the sack, darlings, just to prove there there were *still* no hard feelings.' In Tacoma, sozzled and exhausted, she awoke from a drunken sleep to find it had snowed onto her carpet through her open window. She called room service for a gin and a snow shovel. When the *Little Foxes* finished, she had played 104 cities and covered, as the crow flies, 30,000 miles. Nobody seemed to spot that the bizarre behaviour might have been a mixture of grief, exhaustion and low spirits gamefully fought. Everyone assumed it was just 'Tallulah behaviour'.

Tallulah spent a lot of her time supporting the War Effort with spontaneous personal appearances and rallies and one-off benefits. She also started rehearsing her latest play, Thornton Wilder's *The Skin Of Our Teeth*. It is a truly weird play. Already turned down by a long line of producers who said they could not understand a word of it, it was produced here by Michael Myerbergh, who Tallulah hated. She also hated the director, Elia Kazan, (because he tactfully let her know she was third choice for the role) and his wife Florence Eldridge, because she was a tight-gusseted prude. The rehearsal period was akin to The Great War, but with ruder language. Elia Kazan finally won Tallulah's respect by getting two stage hands to tie her to a chair while he gave her his notes. Eventually, they became allies against the dreaded Myerbergh. In the cast was the sexually uncertain Montgomery Clift, who became close to our star and explored his swinging dilemma by sleeping with both Tallulah and Stephen Cole.

'This is a dauntless and heart-rending comedy that stands head and shoulders above anything ever written for the American stage', decided Alexander Woollcott on the opening of the show. Other crics were similarly enthralled. Tallulah opened with a feather duster as a prop and these lines; 'I hate this play and every single word in it! I don't understand a single word of it and the troubles the human race has gone through. The author hasn't made up his mind if we're living back in the caves, or we're in New Jersey today.' The piece was sufficiently avant-garde to make sotto voce ad lib arguments between its star and Elia Kazan's wife, such as 'Tallulah, be a good girl': 'I'm sick and tired of being a good girl, and what's more, I'm sick and tired of your fucking moaning', seem like part of the fabric of the play. And with Tallulah doing an onstage version of 'There's Less To This Than Meets The Eye', the play was a huge success, playing for 229 performances with Tallulah in it, and when *she* won the Drama Critics Award for Best Actress, and Thornton Wilder won a Pulitzer, he presumably did what playwrights do about successful ad libs, he claimed them as his own.

Tallulah grew tired of her endless hotels and bought a house in Bedford Village. It had seventy windows, and was called ... Windows. She wanted a house to suit her personality and this was it! The world had been looking in

TALLULAH AT HER HOME
'WINDOWS'. THE WORLD
HAD BEEN LOOKING IN ON
HER FOR ALL OF HER ADULT
LIFE. SO ... A HOUSE WITH
SEVENTY WINDOWS

on her for all of her adult life. She did it up in spiffy style, with her Renoirs, Chagalls, Toulouse-Lautrec nicknacks and her Augustus John. Like Farm Street, it was ever-open and ran interminable parties. The job of 'caddying' passed from hand to hand. Stephen Cole to Montgomery Clift to Morton da Costa. Tallulah wrote 'I have three phobias which, if I could mute them, would make my life as slick as a sonnet, but as dull as ditch water: I hate to go to bed, I hate to get up, and I hate to be alone.'

For 'hate' read 'fear'. If she spent her time constantly fending off these three ghouls, her entire life must have been a brave fight. Her weapon, which she wields constantly in these pages, was her sense of humour. Tiny Sword, Fearful Foes.

Now in her forties, Tallulah's character was solidifying into this mould: she needed people around her all the time, she performed almost no caretaking, housekeeping or cleaning jobs herself. She left clothes where they dropped, and all inanimate objects became antagonistic bad props which refused to open, switch on, ring, unscrew, be bought. She *could* light her own cigarettes – but then she hated anyone touching her hands and arms. She needed someone to be there when she slept, and when she woke from sleeping. She wasn't sleeping very well. She was a television addict; the set had to be on all the time. She had stomach ulcers, she had difficulty eating. She was addicted to smoking, bourbon and cocaine. She was addicted to work. The house was full of friends who came to stay the night and were still there two years later. Dogs ran everywhere, and Tallulah, their mistress, was the only one who didn't know how to feed them. She did not seem to be able to manage her money. Either she had a great stash, which she threw around haphazardly, or she was in enormous debt. Sexually, she propositioned anything close by. Male homosexuals thanked her for the romantic proposal and, mostly, fended her off. Male heterosexuals, she stalked. Her caddie/maid/house-guests were put on dressing the bedroom with perfume, candles and drink. Female heterosexuals were brazenly propositioned. Lesbians were stalked, propositioned, befriended and teased. Ex-lovers down on their luck were invited to stay forever. Dola Cavendish stayed so long that Edie Smith moved out in protest.

For The War Effort, she consented to appear in a movie. *Stage Door Canteen*, in 1943, had a simple plot. A brave young American soldier (Lou McAllister) has never been kissed. A patriotic girl, (Marjorie Riordan) kisses him. But not before an awful lot of stars have had cameos. Here is a list of just *some* of them:

Cheryl Walker, Lou McAllister, Judith Anderson, Ray Bolger, Katherine Cornell, Helen Hayes, Alfred Lunt, Harpo Marx, Yehudi Menuhin, Cornelia Otis Skinner, Ethel Waters, Dame May Whitty, William Demarest, Gracie Fields, Katherine Hepburn, Gertrude Lawrence, Ethel Merman, Merle Oberon, Johnny Weismuller, Lynne Fontsanne, Paul Muni, Gypsy Rose Lee, George Raft ... plus the bands Count Basie, Benny Goodman, Xavier Cugat. I have one comment: Yehudi *Menuhin*? James Agee had just one also; 'A nice harmless picture for the whole family, and a goldmine for those who are willing to go to it in the right spirit'. Tallulah gave her fee to The War Effort. She had meant to use it to pay for a cripplingly-expensive pool for Windows, so she agreed to go back to the loathsome movie business and appear in *Lifeboat*.

The film was directed by Alfred Hitchcock and based on a story by John Steinbeck. A German U-boat destroys a passenger ship leaving a lifeboat full of telling stereotypes plus the U-boat commander as a sort of microcosm of life and particularly life with brave and complex Americans and a snivelling, murdering German. The tragic young mother of a dead baby commits suicide, a dance-mad lower-orders type loses a leg, a young black pick-pocket finds God, the goddamm Nazi behaves like a goddamm Nazi *and* he's a coward when push comes to shove and Tallulah, the sophisticated, perfectly coiffured and minked writer Connie Porter, falls for the rough but gorgeous ordinary seaman, John Hodiak. The love-interests of course got it together off-camera, so the sex scenes *sizzled*. Tallulah and Hodiak improvised sexy dialogue with a lot of lipstick-writing-on-bare-chest shenaningans, and the whole thing was filmed on one set in a great water tank. Tallulah wore no underwear for the whole fifteen week shoot and, during the storm sequence, stunningly created by big tubs of hurled water and fake fog, caught pneumonia. Again ... And nearly died. Again.

Afficionados of Hitchcock's signature appearances in his own films will be interested to know that while he was strongly drawn to appearing as a bloated corpse floating past the lifeboat, Less is More prevailed and he appeared as an advertisement for 'Reduco Obesity Slayer', a slimming product, on the back of Connie Porter's newspaper.

The best line was Connie's. As the rescue boat (Allied or German?) approached, Connie spunkily quipped 'Some of my best friends are in concentration camps.'

Tallulah won the Screen Critics Award for Actress Of The Year, but not the Oscar. The film was a fabulous success. Hitler hated it. Of course, suddenly Hollywood was interested again. She was offered *A Royal Scandal* – a deathless tale about the love life of Catherine The Great of Russia, but with the Horse Rumour and the Entire Russian Guard Story non-included.

Greta Garbo, who had retired from screenwork in 1941, and with whom Tallulah had never seen eye to eye, on account of competitive affairs and friendships with the same women, suddenly expressed an interest in playing Catherine. Otto Preminger was director, and because of her good turn in getting him citizenship, was loyal to Tallulah. The producer, Ernst Lubitsch, was a big Garbo fan and *furious*, so he hired Anne Baxter, half Tallulah's age, to play her lady-in-waiting and love rival to William Eythe, the twenty-six year old male lead. The set was another Great War. Eythe was discovered to be *hung* and became Tallulah's caddy. The film was a ridiculuous romp in an improbable Russian court. It did not do well; 'Nothing is one-tenth well enough done, and all the laughs are played for at their cheapest, far down the ramp', wrote James Agee.

Tallulah went back to the stage while she waited for *A Royal Scandal* to open. She must have known. *Foolish Notion*, a thin comedy by Philip Barry, had poor responses on the try-outs and even worse ones in town. The only remarkable thing about the run was that she was reunited in Thespis with her ex-husband and they became friends again.

In her forties, she started to spend time again with her sister. Eugenia had 'prayed in every church in Europe for a baby', and God had overheard in one of them and let her adopt a baby, William Brockman, known as Billy. Billy had blue eyes like his namesake. Tallulah invited Eugenia to Windows to visit, and fell in love with her nephew. She made a great aunt for a boy, spoiling him rotten, buying him expensive presents, dancing with him, reading to him, cuddling him and handing him back to his mother in the evenings. Eugenia and Tallulah competed as usual, with Eugenia claiming the fulfilled mother and wife Prize (she was on husband number seven) and Tallulah stepping up for the Legend-In-My-Own-Lifetime Prize. Playing Sisters-Get-On, they both answered questions in a magazine article on 'Are You An Alcoholic?' Tallulah, filling in the answers carefully, discovered that Eugenia was, indeed, an alcoholic.

In 1946, Tallulah became interested in reviving a fifteen year old play, *Private Lives*. It had been a tremendous success in London with Noel Coward, Gertrude Lawrence and Laurence Olivier in it. Tallulah said she only played it to escape debtor's prison but she must have felt in her waters that Amanda Prynne, jacking in her groom of one day to run off with Eliot, her first husband, who is on honeymoon with *his* second wife and has appeared on the adjoining balcony, was another fantastic vehicle for her. Her co-star was Donald Cook, who had been hopelessly alcoholic in *Foolish Notion*, and was now declared dry. Alas, the combination of out-of-town tour, and Tallulah, set him off drinking again.

In 1947, Tallulah appeared in a short run of an Americanisation of a Jean Cocteau piece *La Mort Ecoute Aux Portes*. This is remarkable only in that the heroine delivers a 20,000 word opening speech before being shot by the young assassin she has fallen in love with. Oh, and Tallulah insisting on the management employing a new, interesting young actor as the assassin: Marlon Brando. The two leads, and their acting styles, did not get on. Marlon Brando was replaced. Entitled *The Eagle Has Two Heads*, critics dubbed it *The Turkey Has Two Heads*. 47 performances only.

Private Lives resumed touring at Westport, Connecticut, on 14 July 1948. Tallulah was Amanda Prynne every show-night for 204 weeks. The Gallery Girls returned, thrilled at the perfect Tallulah vehicle. On some nights, she actually performed *some* of the author's text. Donald Cook, as Eliot, was often drunk. So, too, was Tallulah, but, 'In all my years in the theatre I've never missed a performance because of alcoholic wounds. I have never skidded into the footlights through confused vision. No curtain has been prematurely lowered on a play of mine that the litter-bearers might get an emergency workout.' Well, no, Tallulah, but were the performances *always* unaffected other than by nerves?

Coward came to see the show in Chicago, so the cast agreed to put back all his lines. Coward was delighted with the show and agreed to let it go to Broadway (as if, with Broadway royalties, he's going to say 'no'). The performers returned to ad libbing, fighting on stage and complicated interconnecting on-the-road affairs (which explained the onstage fighting).

Tallulah got severe pains in her shoulder, was diagnosed with neuritis, and put in traction. The show closed for two weeks, during which Donald Cook was ordered to dry out. Then on to Minneapolis, Cincinnati, Cleveland, Pittsburgh, Kansas, St Louis, San Fransisco, Los Angeles – and those were just the towns whose names you'd recognise.

During this gruelling schedule, Tallulah found time to be The Celebrity Voter for Harry S. Truman's race for The White House. She recorded a three-minute speech in the interval of *Private Lives* from her dressing-room. 'I would be faithless to Alabama, did I not vote for Harry Truman. Yes, I'm for Harry Truman, the human being. By the same token I'm against Thomas E. Dewey, the mechanical man!' The speech was witty, persuasive and sincere. Dewey tried to have it censored before it went out. In the battle-royal which ensued, the speech was printed in its entirety in every major newspaper in America. Truman won, the Tinman lost. *Private Lives* went to Broadway on 4 October 1948. It played at the Plymouth Theater for 248 nights.

The Press responded by misrepresenting some of her actions. She was accused of gate-crashing a presidential ceremony – she was photographed kissing Truman's hand with the caption 'HE'S HER MAN!!' She sued. In each case she got a printed apology. No damages. Wasn't interested.

She *was* interested to sue when Prell shampoo ran a radio jingle which ran 'I'm Tallulah, the tube of Prell, and I've got a little something to sell'. She refused to be a tube of hair product. 'I've yet to endorse a floor wax, a flea powder, or wart remover, a cigar or hookah pipe'. She sued Proctor and Gamble Etc. for $1,000,000. She settled out of court for $5,000.

Another brush with the law ended less well. At Marblehead, Massachusett, two young policemen were called to quieten down the last-night party. Tallulah, out of her skull, naked and smoking a joint got into a fist fight with one of them. They dragged her screaming and kicking, for a night in lock-up. *Very* Sybil Thorndike.

And finally, in a decade of legal complications, Evelyn Cronin, her sixty-year old maid was caught redhanded kiting cheques, signed by Tallulah, with a few extra noughts added by Evelyn. Tallulah tried to convince the authorities that the incident had been a one-off aberration in a heretofore unblemished maiding career, even though it wasn't, and Evelyn had in fact been stealing from her on a regular basis. Tallulah's accountant, a brave man, insisted on a full inquiry. Tallulah refused to take it to court. Evelyn packed her bags and left Tallulah's employment. Tallulah recounted the story to newspaper columnist Walter Winchell who ran it as a story. The District Attorney got wind of it, and the case went to trial.

The play now toured the South, with Tallulah cheerfully adding the *Gone With The Wind* line 'Frankly my dear, I don't give a damn' to the now thoroughly mongrelised text. Both Tallulah and Donald Cook were drinking heavily, before, during and after the curtain. Blocked to roll off the sofa while fighting, they were often too sozzled to negotiate their climb back on. By now, they hated one another and their backstage fights would often be heard heralding their entrances, and their onstage textual fights were enhanced by details of their private squabbles. Art and Life were now interchangeable.

On 3 June 1950, in Passaic, New Jersey, Tallulah said 'I've had enough. I'm never going to act in the theatre again, I swear.' That was it. She had finished with *Private Lives* forever. She finished the forties exhausted. And with an embarassing and upsetting trial ahead of her ...

Girlfriend, district attorney and Driving Miss Daisy

In *The First Wives' Club*, Goldie Hawn's character, a movie actress of a certain age, says that a female actress's career has three stages: girlfriend, district attorney, and Driving Miss Daisy. It is a very funny line because it is very true. Hollywood believes, in the face of overwhelming evidence, that women live only to find a cute man, that they don't hold down *real* jobs, and when something dangerous happens, they turn into blancmanges and cannot do anything but scream in loud (but high) decibels, while the *man* gets on with fist-fights, shooting and blowing up perfectly good buildings. It also believes, except when it's making a *controversial* movie, that what attracts young, beautiful women is a man in his late fifties or early sixties. *Nobody* ever has a relationship with any woman who has a less-than-model-girl figure. While men *occasionally* get attracted to each other, women hardly ever do. Anybody porky, wrinkly, unusually-featured becomes nurse, secretary, burger waitress, mother, murdering bitch, or crowd. That's how Hollywood portrays life. And Theatre isn't that far behind on this one.

Which leaves actresses over forty with a very narrow window of opportunity. Which leaves radio.

Tallulah had been making radio already; *Twelfth Night, 1937*; *The Talley Method*, *The Little Foxes* and *Suspicion* in 1941; *I Served On Bataan*, 1943; *These Are Our Men, A Salute To The U.S.* and *Cruiser Helena* in 1945 and *The Story of Helen Zabriskie* in 1946. Radio had been hugely popular during the twenties and thirties, but with the advent of television it was losing its public in great stampedes to the small screen. Columbia Broadcasting Company had raided a lot of NBC's personnel and handcuffed them with long-term contracts. What to do? Tallulah explains it thus: 'In rebuttal they decided to group into a Sunday night show such an outlay of stars that no man, woman or child in the nation would be so foolish as to listen to anything else in the interval between 6.30 and 8.00p.m. Eastern Standard Time.'

So NBC launched, with a massive budget of $50,000 per show, a ninety-minute flagship Sunday-evening radio variety show with a big array of glittering stars, called *The Big Show*. Ten per cent of the budget would be spent on the presenter's fee. NBC offered it to Tallulah. The idea, startlingly innovative in its day, was that Tallulah would simply be herself. Yes, a Personality. Dee Englebach was the unsuspecting producer, Goodman Ace and Frank Wilson would write the script and ad libs, and weekly guests would be introduced and chatted to by Tallulah. She was sick with dread. The most frightening job any actor could imagine was to 'just be yourself'. The radio hosts of the forties coated their introductions with sugar and honey; Tallulah delivered hers steeped in jolly venom. Ethel Merman was to headline the first show, with a support cast of Frankie Laine, Jimmy Durante, Danny Thomas and Portland Hoffa. Merman arrived wanting to do six songs, but was whittled down to four. The first show broadcast on 4 November 1950. Anita Loos sent a telegram saying 'THE DAY YOU GO ON THE RADIO SHOULD BE DECLARED A NATIONAL HOLIDAY.'

The rehearsals went badly. Tallulah was under-confident because she felt like an interloper, a dramatic actress in the middle of variety turns. Her readings sounded dreary and under-energised. This was because she was so frightened, if she'd given it any emotional welly, she would have burst into tears and been labelled 'difficult'. The producer and management were white – worried and glad that they only had her on a four-show contract. Only William Joyce, her agent at William Morris said 'You don't know Tallulah. She doesn't give out at rehearsals. Wait until she goes on air.'

Sick with dread, at six o'clock Sunday 4 November, Tallulah went out live: Jimmy Durante, who, like the others, could see her shaking , whispered 'Remember payday, baby.' ...

'NBC Bigwigs were ready to jump off a cliff. Me? I'd jump from my own cliff. In my leap, I'd need no collaborators!' An audience of 30,000,000 listened in. The opening programme of *The Big Show* was, to one critic, 'the fastest and funniest ninety minutes in my memory'. Tallulah's autopsy was delayed. John Crosby, in The *Herald Tribune*, wrote: 'However, NBC's biggest gamble may have been Tallulah Bankhead, an unpredictable volcano who has been known to sweep away whole villages when she erputs. As mistress of ceremonies, though, she was sharp as a knife and succeeded somehow in outshining even the most glittering names on that glittering roster. Tallulah is more or less iconoclastic, if that's not too mild a word, and consequently the passages between her and her guests were happily lacking in that overwhelming mutual esteem which marks the pleasantries between most MCs and guests. Tallulah even sang 'Give My Regards To Broadway' in a voice that almost had more timbre than Yellowstone National Park.'

Now that's what I *call* a Review!

Ethel Merman was rounded off with 'Thank you, Ethel darling. That was wonderful – and may I say, you don't look a day over sixty!' Portland Hoffa got the hugest laugh by addressing Tallulah as 'Sir'. The comedy was always the comedy of insult. Guests were always viewed in terms of their approaching old age, their diminishing looks, diminution of sexual prowess, lack of earning ability and ever-increasing drinking, which was always capped by Tallulah's approaching old age, diminishing looks, etc., etc. The jokes were burlesque: 'Did your mother see me? She never could', 'No mews is good Mews', Tannhauser, it used to be Fivehauser, but inflation set in', 'That gown you have on. What colour is it? Well, it's a new colour, battleship grey. Battleship grey? It's lovely. But isn't it just a little tight around the boiler room?' (this was in a sketch between Marlene Dietrich and Tallulah).

For over two years, *The Big Show* was the most popular and talked-about show on American radio. Guests included Fanny Brice, Lauritz Melchior, Clifton Webb, Douglas Fairbanks Jr, Gloria Swanson, Edith Piaf, Judy Garland, Gary Cooper, and Marlene Dietrich.

Tallulah referred to the *Big Show* production team as 'my boys' and behaved like a loosey-goosey Mother towards them, even going so far as to slap Jerry

TALLULAH WITH NAT KING
COLE, ONE OF HER GUESTS
ON 'THE BIG SHOW'

Lewis' face (Oh *Good!*) for being unpleasant to them. 'That's for being rude to my boys, you no-good son-of-a-bitch!'

The Big Show continued to thrive through 1950 and 1951, with Billy Ecksteine, Eddie Cantor, Carmen Miranda, Fred Allen among the starry guests. High-pitch-voiced Earl Wilson asked if Tallulah had ever been mistaken for a man over the radio: 'Never darling, have you?' Tallulah has some claims to the title 'Can I do camp? Darling ... I *invented* it'.

On the back of this triumph, Tallulah got to do radio productions of *Dark Victory* and *Humoresque* in 1951 *All About Eve* in 1952 and *Hedda Gabler* in 1954. She was drinking heavily. Some of her gay male hanger-abouts often played a good game with her. It consisted of persuading her to have just one more for the road and then just one more for the ... It was called getting Tallulah swacked. In June 1951, Tallulah was rushed to hospital, this time with an infected gall-bladder. It was in hospital, while being told to take it easy that it occurred to her to take *The Big Show* for a one-off to England. Whenever she got ill, her instinct seems to have been to double her work and stress load. After all, if you stop working, who are you? Nobody.

Tallulah arrived in London to record an English *The Big Show* after an emergency landing at Shannon Airport with no dogs ('your goddam quarantine regulations') wearing a pink chamois leather suit 'just the thing for comfortable flying' and a lot of jewellery. She was looking after her gall-bladder condition by drinking black coffee, not eating, and smoking a whole pack of cigarettes at one sitting. She breezed through customs and interviews on a phalanx of quips, insults and sexual innuendo, after a flight of far too many hours in a pink chamois suit – 'Isn't it just shattering, darlings, having an engine steal your thunder? And isn't your princess and her little ones so absolutely adorable?' Despite being absent from these shores for nearly twenty years, waiting for her were over a hundred Gallery Girls, older, bigger, wrinkled ...

The English edition of *The Big Show* was recorded at The Palladium to Huge Applause. Tallulah began with 'Bless you darlings! Now, let me see. What was I saying when I left England sixteen years ago? Oh yes – make mine a double!' Her guests were Beatrice Lillie, George Sanders, Jack Buchanan, Vera Lynn, Robb Wilto and England's Glamour ShowBiz Couple Vivien Leigh and Laurence Olivier. Tallulah was adorably pleasant to MGM's choice for Scarlett O'Hara, but she had a good time exploring her fabled hatred of Bette Davis, who had now shot *another* arrow into Tallulah's pioneer chest by adding the role of Margo Channing in *All About Eve* to the parts she had snatched from Tallulah.

> '*Do you think I don't* know *who's been spreading gossip about me and my temperament out there in Hollywood, darlings? Where they made that film* All About Me? *After all the nice things I've said about that hag, Bette Davis? When I get hold of her, I'll tear every hair out of her moustache!*'

If Tallulah sounds like a Drag Queen here, we must remember that this stuff was *scripted*. By male writers out for laughs. Donald Cook during a late-night drinking and talking session on the interminable *Private Lives* tour had been asked by Stephen Cole what would become of Tallulah. 'She'll end up like Jack Barrymore, a caricature of herself.' She was now playing the part of *herself* which has its advantages; someone writes your scripts for you, and its disadvantages; you don't get a day off. You have to be more *you* than you. And when people have views on your performance, you cannot say 'well, they don't like me as Hamlet, Lady Macbeth, Amanda Elliott, but I'm still me.' She was a Personality, and the critics didn't like her; 'Miss Bankhead begins her season, still billed as "glamorous and unpredictable". She is definitely no longer the second. Her vain, rude and temperamental role has worn very thin. She would be well advised to try something fresh.'

She flew to Paris for the French edition of *The Big Show*. Le Grand – er – Show. Broadcast on 23 September, from The Empire, Tallulah enchanted everyone by her fluency – one of her guests, Mistinguett, now seventy-five said 'you are probably the only woman in the world who has handled more pricks than I have, on *and* off the stage.' The guests were a British/French mix; Gracie Fields, Georges Guetary, Françoise Rosay and Joan Fontaine. And Tallulah's Personality in France? – *France Soir* described her as 'The great, irresistible one who resembles a Sunday-school teacher" – France-Soir.

I think they must do Sunday school differently in Paris.

On returning to New York, Tallulah announced her intention to write her autobiography. Up and down the continent, faces blenched. This was the fifties when all the Western World was just one big padlocked Closet. She got herself a state-of-the-art tape recorder and began to spill. She took as her starting point Edna St Vincent Millay's lines:

> My candle burns at both ends
> It will not last the night;
> But oh, my foes, and ah, my friends
> It gives a lovely light.

Tallulah was now on about 150 cigarettes a day, and one-to-two bottles of bourbon. If you wonder whether civilisation has advanced at all, consider the advent of Alcoholics and Narcotics Anonymous, think about Betty Ford and The Priory.

But her own private life was about to become public once again. She probably had huge nerves about The Evelyn Cronin trial, and those nerves needed anaesthetising. The trial, not surprisingly, attracted huge coverage. The brief for Evelyn Cronin adopted a 'simple, loving maid corrupted by decadent star' approach. The defence asserted that Tallulah had taught Cronin how to roll joints, had her procure for her and that Tallulah beat her at least fifty times. Tallulah's lifestyle was established as one of drinking, smoking, taking cocaine and having to buy sex. 'The next thing they'll have me vivisecting my fucking dogs!' raged Tallulah. The prosecution established the 'she was a stripper in burlesque, sure she's guilty' approach. In between hurling insults and name-blackening, the case *was* established against Evelyn Cronin. She did *kite* cheques and was found guilty on three charges of grand larceny. She was bailed for $1,000 and then given a one-to-two year prison sentence. Tallulah pleaded for clemency, asking for her former maid's age and health to be taken into consideration. The prison sentence was dropped. Tallulah filed a suit against her accountant for not exercising due care and attention of her funds and the whole thing settled down. Evelyn Cronin died in May 1953 when she was sixty-one, a year after the court case. Tallulah felt deep remorse about the whole sideshow for the rest of her life.

When her autobiography *Tallulah*, came out, it became a bestseller, and was serialised in 30 American newspapers and many others worldwide, including, in Britain, The *Express*. It is a funny, forgiving, generous book which never for one moment lets anybody anywhere near her centre. Like her personality on *The Big Show*, it was ghost-written by a man, Richard Maney. It is big on details about her sex life with men, coy and vague about the women she slept with. It also sets her up as eternally sassy, quick-witted and ironic. Essence of Camp Icon.

The publicity engendered by the autobiography led to an offer to do a cabaret act at The Sands Hotel, Las Vegas. At $20,000 a week, the offer was too good to turn down. Her current caddie and lover, Patsy Kelly, an actress from the Hal Roach comedies, went with her instead of Edie Smith, who was exhausted and Glenn Anders, who was afraid, because of adverse publicity, of being seen as her pimp. Wearing a white low-cut gown, and long black gloves, Tallulah presented a version of herself written by male writers, the fabulous, naughty drunk-druggie encountering real life. It was a huge success. And Tallulah added another addiction to her bag – gambling in the casino.

Next she returned to movie work. Instead of a character, she played herself in *Main Street To Broadway*, a Lester Cowan Production in which, after many reverses a young playwright sees his work through to a Broadway opening night. It fails, but he has learned several lessons (opening a show *and* learning lessons? that's a Bridge Too Far for a playwright!). It was an unsuccessful, flat attempt to show the public how Broadway works, with big stars playing themselves in cameo roles. Written by Samuel Raphaelson, directed by Tay Garnett and produced by James Wong Howe, the star cameos included Tom Morton, Mary Murphy, Ethel Barrymore, Lionel Barrymore, Shirley Booth, Rex Harrison, Lilli Palmer, Helen Hayes, Henry Fonda, Mary Martin, Louis Calhern, John Van Druten, Cornel Wilde, Joshua Logan, Agnes Moorehead and Gertrude Berg. It was remarkable only for her encounter with a young, unknown James Dean. They arranged a date, which Dean did not turn up for, but while she was making her first television, *Hedda Gabler*, she ran into him in the corridor. Both impressive Bad Behaviour fans, they immediately pretended to have sex with each other right there and then, she hiking up her skirt and wrapping her legs round his. He took her out on a date 'You remind me of Edith Piaf . She's another prima-donna bitch who gives me a hard-on.' 'I got to play his bongos', said Tallulah. She never saw him again. On his death she said 'God has taken away one of His most talented children.'

She returned to the New York stage in 1954 as a middle-aged matriarch with *Dear Charles*, by Arthur Penn. Critics decided it was a rather average production, but redeemed by Tallulah: 'the play was appalling for this day and age, but it's difficult to remain honestly appalled when you are rapt with admiration.' The Gallery Girls were still shrieking. They shrieked for 155 performances.

This was followed, at last by the role we all *really* wanted to see Tallulah in; Blanche in *A Streetcar Named Desire*. Homophobes dropping a bomb at the premiere would have wiped out most of New York's gay men, here to see somebody they called 'The Queens' Queen'. Various Tennessee Williams lines such as 'The girls are out tonight', were adopted as instant Polare and Tallulah decided that now she 'had Gallery Girls of Both Sexes!' Wolcott Gibbs wrote 'There is, I suppose, no cure for this kind of vulgarity and stupidity in an audience, except possibly the brisk employment of a machine gun'. Ah, Wolcott, how right you are. Tallulah welcomed her new gay darlings with a camp review entitled 'Welcome Darlings!' which consisted of two acts and twenty-six sketches, and included Tallulah as Peter Pan, ('I am Peter Pan, darling') which brought the house down, Tallulah singing 'I've heard a lot about you' and reciting Dorothy Parker's *The Waltz*. It continued her *Big Show* wisecracking, camp persona.

With her advancing years, the fact that she still enjoyed flinging off her clothes to make a party go, happily peeing in front of people and continually propositioning all ages and all sexes, made her seem even more outrageous. She was still drinking heavily, and the cigarette smoking made stairs difficult. She got lots of health warnings, which she ignored. Now with emphysema, she gave up smoking, then started again, then gave up, then started again. She needed dressing-rooms by the stage at every venue. At fifty-three, close up, she looked frail and ill. In full slap, from a stage, or in a photograph however, she still looked knockout. She took up a new caddie, Jimmy Kirkwood, who would eventually make his name with *A Chorus Line*.

Tallulah moved onto *Eugenia*, which she accepted without reading because the name was lucky, on account of it being her sister's and Eugenia Rawls. She played a wicked fortune-hunter who creates mayhem for every sweet sucker in the cast and then gets her come-uppance just before the curtain. Tallulah wouldn't wear glasses despite the fifty-something eyesight and with her drinking she proved an accident-rich zone throughout the tour. She broke a finger on a set, tripped, and with a drugload of bourbon, Tuinal, Dexedrine, Benzedrine and Dexamyl inside her, her performances, unsurprisingly, tended to dry up. At one point, she started saying lines from *The Little Foxes*. When she couldn't be found for a Saturday matinee, and they finally tracked her down, off her head in her bath, the producers closed the play. It didn't make it into town.

She took *Welcome Darlings* to London, hitting town with a salvo of putdowns about her great age and declining looks; 'don't photograph my arse, it looks like an accordion! Photograph down, darling. That's how they made Shirley Temple look beautiful. They used to shoot her through gauze, but they shoot me through *linoleum!*' and 'My new hat, darling. It's to cover my grey hairs!' On her return she was on the Personality Circuit, appearing on television talk-shows camping herself and her memories up. Sometimes she sang, mostly she talked and gave good personality. *The Arthur Murray Party*, *The Polly Bergen Show*, even Be Still My Heart, *The Lucy and Des Show*. She made two television plays, *The Hole Card* and *Eyes Of A Stranger*, directed by Ray Milland. She did a summer-circuit tour of *House On The Rocks*, which she described as 'a dead duck'. Then she agreed to do *Crazy October*, the attractions of which were Estelle Winwood as co-star, and the fact that it was black, camp and that she was paid a salary of $1,500 a week, plus fifteen per cent of the box-office.

Her health was poor, her temper uncertain and her behaviour increasingly off-the-wall as she toured *Crazy October*, then did *Midgie Purvis*, for which she was nominated for a Tony, but which got duff reviews and closed after 21 nights. She was having a lot of 'accidents' which is code for being drunk . She got hooked on occultism and started trying to contact her mother . She fell asleep with a cigarette burning in her hand and to kill the pain, took more drugs. These gave her hallucinations so she thought her apartment was being invaded by intruders. Her staff and her new caddie, Ted Hook, were finding her more and more difficult to live with.

In Spring 1963, she turned down the Joan Crawford role opposite Bette Davis in *Whatever Happened To Baby Jane*. Big mistake. Instead, she agreed to be Flora Goforth in *The Milk Train Doesn't Stop Here Anymore*, by Tennessee Williams, because 'A promiscuous, pill-ravaged rip, born in a Georgia swamp? That could only possibly be me!' Her leading man was, get this, Tab Hunter! They did not get on. Tab Hunter had as foul a mouth as Tallulah but droned on about, a) himself and, b) horses. The play opened in Baltimore and the first act speeches were syncopated by the sound of flipped seats as the audience walked out. Tony Richardson jumped ship as the production went into New York. Everybody was gathered to catch Tallulah falling. Rumours abounded that she was drinking her way through the play and everybody wanted to see it. David Merrick wrote 'Miss Bankhead was hoarse and unhappy.' That was the entire review. The reviews, and President Kennedy's shooting, closed the show after 5 nights. Tallulah said she hated the stage anyway, but Tennessee Williams noticed 'She loves the theatre with so much of her heart that, in order to protect her heart, she has to say she hates it.' It was her last appearance on Broadway.

Her last appearance on film was in *Die! Die! My Darling!* A Hammer Horror Film. Here is its *Halliwell Filmgoers Companion*'s entry:

> 'An American girl in England visits the mother of her dead fiancé and finds herself the prisoner of a religious maniac. Boringly overlong Grand Guignol, which even defeats its gallantly unmade up and deathly-looking star; mildly notable as a record of one of her last performances. w. Richard Matheson, novel Nightmare, Anne Blaisdell d. Silvio Narizzano, Tallulah Bankhead, Stefanie Powers, Peter Vaughan, Yootha Joyce and Donald Sutherland.'

(Can you put those names together in one film experience?) Tallulah played Mrs Trefoile, a religious fanatic gone bats at the death of her only son. Tallulah thought to jump on the currently hot Hammer Horror bandwagon. She sent a production still of herself to her friend Cal Schumann with 'Who dat? Not me. Oh well. Tallulah!' She suddenly looked old. She was now in the *Driving Miss Daisy* time of a movie actress' life. She was offered more like roles. She turned them all down and went to earth, emerging only to appear in the odd television appearance or do a voice-over. She acquired yet another new caddie, Jesse Levy who was forty-five.

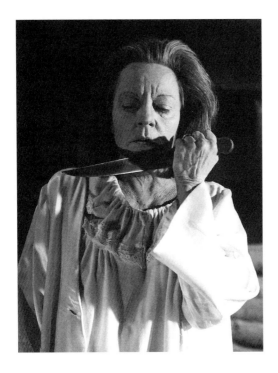

DIE! DIE! MY DARLING!
— TALLULAH BARELY
RECOGNISED HERSELF

When she was offered The Black Widow in the gloriously cardboard *Batman* series, and told she would have to be camp, she said she would have no problem with that. She was its mother. She now needed an oxygen inhaler on hand and her feet and legs were swollen from barbiturate misuse.

She inhaled enough oxygen to row with Lena Horne over her autobiography, in which she claimed Tallulah had referred to 'piccanninnies' . Tallulah called Lena Horne a 'lying bitch'.

She appeared on *The Smothers Brothers Show* but her rendition of 'My Funny Valentine' was cut to make way for a number by Cass Elliott, of The Mamas and The Papas. She appeared on *The Merv Griffins Show* to prove to 'all my fans that I'm not dead, darling'. On 14 May, she was on *The Tonight Show* with McCartney and Lennon, where she declared herself incapable of understanding their lyrics; 'Too much social significance', and that the love of her life was actually ... baseball.

Baseball?

It would all soon be over.

CHEERING ON THE NEW YORK GIANTS AT A BASEBALL GAME,
THE LOVE OF HER LIFE

Curtain

Wagner: *'I have been feeling like shit.*
My belly always seems like it's got a dead rat
rolling around in it.
I jump at the slightest sound.
The palms of my hands are slick and hot with sweat.
Thirteen times now has my face broken out in an angry
red sea of yellow-headed pimples, aching red spots
and shoal upon shoal of blackheads.
I feel stagnant. I feel like a slimy green pond
in the middle of a dark wood. I feel like stale soup.'

Tallulah Bankhead died during the night of 12 December 1968.

The woman whose life began as the Wright Brothers made their first flight, and as women's suffrage started it's long fight, ended in a year like this:

The Americans were fighting the Vietnam War. The Tet Offensive attacked Saigon. Millions of lives were lost. Lyndon B. Johnston stopped wholesale bombing. The American people along with the rest of the world, were becoming disillusioned with the point of the Vietnam War. Robert Kennedy, the hope of the Democrats, was running for nomination to the Presidential Election Race, when he was gunned down at The Ambassador's Hotel, Los Angeles by a mysterious gunman. For twenty-five hours he clung to life in The Good Samaritans hospital and then he, like his brother John before him, died, assassinated. It was the Year of the student barricades, in Paris, London and

America. Martin Luther King led a huge rally to Washington, addressing the mass crowd at the Lincoln Memorial. He too was assassinated by a lone gunman.

Russia and Czechoslovakia met to deal with Russia's worries over the loyalty of Czechoslovakia, and her desire for reform and the creation of socialism with a new human face. Six weeks later, Russian tanks trundled up the streets of Prague. Dubcek was arrested. Someone put a single red rose in the barrel of one of the tank's huge guns. Yuri Gagarin, the first space astronaut, dies in a plane crash. Valentina Tereschcova, the first woman astronaut, attends his funeral. Roman Polanski marries actress Sharon Tate. He encourages her to continue working, saying he would rather his wife be a hippy than a housewife.

There are race riots.

Apollo 7 splashes down with its three spacemen. The race to the moon is on. In London, it is The Swinging Sixties. The Beatles take a break from Beatlemania to meditate in North India with the Mahareshi Yogi. At the Mexico City Olympics, doves are released as the eternal torch is lit. Hope for everlasting peace. Tom Jones receives a gold disc for his million-seller 'Delilah'.

And Tallulah Bankhead is dying.

Of emphysema.

> Dictionary definition: *[mod. L., Gr. inflation, to puff up] 'The swelling of a part caused by the presence of air in the interstices of the connective tissue' (Syd. Soc. lex) Also the usual sense of the unqualified word), an enlargement of the air vesicles of the lungs (pulmonary or vesicular emphysema.*[14]

> *'It is so easy to take breathing for granted. Breathing is a fully automatic process, beginning at birth and continuing without interruption until the day we die. More to the point, it can be a fully unconscious process – there is no need to attend consciously in any way one's breathing. Just as you can expect to breathe quite*

adequately while sleeping each night, so can we expect our breathing to continue without ever actually doing it. It is the nature of breath that it will continue through the deepest and most unconscious of human sleep.'[15]

Unless you have emphysema.

Tallulah, now living in an apartment, and addicted to soap operas along with everything else was glued to afternoon television when, without warning, inexplicably, her ceiling fell in. It was a Metaphor. While her living room ceiling was being replastered, Tallulah and Jesse, her final caddie, went to live at Rock Hall, Maryland, in Eugenia's guest cottage. Tamara Gevy was a neighbour, Louise Carpenter owned a nearby estate. She invited them to go shooting with her, but Tallulah preferred to play bridge, drink, have dinner with Tamara, and fight with Eugenia. Cindy Brockman brought her two children, Mary Eugenia, four and Tallulah, one, to visit. Tallulah said 'the bitch'd better have blue eyes.' The bitch did. Phew!

She returned to New York, where there was an Asian flu epidemic. Tallulah, tired out and frail, caught it with both hands. Eugenia quotes her as saying 'I'm through and I know it and I don't care any more. Each night when I go to bed, I pray to God that I won't wake up in the morning.' 'Which God?' asked Eugenia, 'The one you don't believe in?' Jesse called the doctor, who rushed her into St Luke's. Tallulah went quietly. She had stopped eating. She was diagnosed with pneumonia. At first she seemed to be doing okay, complaining, screaming, and trying to pull out her intavenous tube. Then the fight went out of her. Her breathing failed and she was taken into intensive care and put on a ventilator. She went into a coma, and died shortly afterwards.

It is reputed that her last audible words were 'Codeine. Bourbon.'

That is: kill pain, kill thought.

The big surprise about her estate was that she left in excess of $2,000,000. Jesse Levy inherited a quarter of that sum, plus the grand piano. Eugenia

Rawls Seawell and her children got half the estate and the remainder went to Eugenia's two grandchildren. Sister got $5,000, a mink coat and $250 a month for life. Estelle Winwood, Kenneth Carten, Philip Hall and Edie Smith got $10,000 each. Jewellery also to the women. Jock Whitney had to buy the Augustus John which Tallulah had promised him.

There was a post mortem. Her liver was in good condition, her lungs were three-quarters clogged with emphysema. If she had given up smoking, this condition would almost certainly have improved and she would have lived.

The funeral took place on 14 December at St Paul's Episcopal Church. The coffin was lined in baby-blue silk for a luxurious ride, Tallulah wore a favourite cigarette-burn-studded bedwrap for a comfy ride. Louisa Carpenter put in Daddy's lucky rabbit's foot. The flowers were white chrysanthemums. A flock of geese quack-quacked overhead as she was buried by the lakeside. Her gravestone bears only her name and the dates of her birth and death.

Nancy Nillson, visiting her grave, remembers:

> *'I remembered she said that what she wanted written on her tombstone was 'Press On'. I took out my lipstick and just before writing those words on that plain, cold granite, Dex, my husband, suggested perhaps the local folk might not appreciate it. I wanted to do it anyway, but I didn't. I did, however, speak to her and said 'Press On, Lady, Press On!'*

Tallulah gave her best epitaph. 'The only thing I regret about my past is the length of it. If I had to live my life again, I'd make the same mistakes, only sooner.'

Well, what are today's Gallery Girls watching? They get dressed up in cowboy gear and watch k.d.lang. They go to stand-up gigs and listen to Donna McPhail, Rhona Cameron, Lea Delaria, Janice Perry, Maria Esposito, Jackie Clune, Suzanne Westenhoeffer, Sabrina Matthews, Marga Gomez, Suzy Berger, Lisa Geduldig, Karen Williams, Lea Delaria and Kate Clinton.

On television they have Ellen DeGeneres, *finally*, coming out! Sandra Bernhard in *Roseanne*. Anne Heche, in movies, playing heterosexual love interests. Madonna ... on and off.

Writing for them are Sarah Daniels, Phyllis Nagy, Sarah Kane, Maya Chowdry, Adrienne Rich ... me ...

Breath always comes in pairs. The In-breath, and the Out-breath. Except at Birth and Death. Tallulah Bankhead expelled that single breath long before I thought of writing at all. Now, on the notice-board of my workroom, I have pinned various wise sayings from other writers, and the one that particularly catches my eye is by Pascal: 'the highest education teaches you to sit alone in a room in silence.' Well, that's what I have been doing writing this book about Tallulah Bankhead. Like History, Biography is a Fiction. Like Fiction, it should bear a Truth. My knowledge of my subject comes from the pages of books, the recorded impressions of her friends and foes, of her family and colleagues. I have only seen her on celluloid. I have only heard her voice on crackly recordings, sitting alone with her in a room. I think she never sat alone in a room in silence. I don't know why. My educated guess is that it terrified her. All my mind and heart tell me that her cigarettes and cocaine and bourbon and work and partying and fucking were her medicine against terror. Her lovely, energetic, soaring humour was designed as a shield to stop people seeing her as anything but coping, managing, getting by. Which is what camp is.

'The whole point about Tallulah', said Hitchcock 'was that she had no inhibitions.' I think what she had were no boundaries. They weren't in place in her childhood and adolescence, and nothing in her choice of career and lifestyle taught her them. If she didn't invent camp, she was certainly one of its earliest practitioners, and technicians. If a lot of her personality was written for her, the uncut gems were her own. I started off doing this book because she made me laugh. By the end I was still laughing, but I was moved as well. Anxious for her. Concerned. Fond. I wish I had seen her in more of those awful plays. I wish she had got better parts. I wish she had been happier, because, although I think she had a lot of *fun*, she didn't seem to have that continuous, supporting happiness. Or is that *contentment?* I don't know. I think she went along with being a Personality because she found it hard work living as a Person. I thought about ending with some sensitive last quote, but here is a favourite joke of hers instead:

Two teenage girls on a Fifth Avenue Bus. One asks the other what she is reading:

> 'The Well Of Loneliness.'
> *'What's it about?'*
> *'Lesbians.'*
> *'What's lesbians?'*
> 'Oh, you know. People like Billie Holiday, Rosalind Russell, Cary Grant.'[15]

Makes me laugh.

Acknowledgments

I have borrowed *shamelessly* from *Tallulah Bankhead: A Scandalous Life*, by David Bret, *Miss Tallulah Bankhead*, by Lee Israel and, of course *Tallulah*, by Tallulah herself. I've scoured *Hollywood Babylon I* and *-II* by Kenneth Anger, and *The Sewing Circle* by Axel Madsen and thrilled at the number of Hollywood and Broadway lesbians and gays both books have outed to me. I have combed the Internet for Bankhead references. There are over *seven hundred* Tallulah pages and mentions, some of them *wonderfully* bizarre. I recommend a late-night surf to you.

I thought a lot about plays and actors and the theatre world. The books that helped me were; David Mamet's *True and False: Heresy and Common Sense for The Actor* is terrific on what acting is. *Improvisation* by Keith Johnstone is a weird, wondrous read on originality, Noel Coward's *Past Imperfect*, and *Acts of Passion, Sexuality, Gender and Performance*, ed. Maya Chowdry and Nina Rapi started me thinking about the handing-on of torches in The Funny Women Olympics. Thinking about Tallulah's approach to health, addiction and dying, I went to *How We Die* by Sherwin B. Nuland, *Meetings At The Edge* by Stephen Levine, *Death, The Final Stage Of Growth* by Elizabeth Kubler-Ross, and *Breathing* by Michael Sky. When I trawled through my childhood giggles and word learning, I had lots of fun with the *Round The Horne Scripts*, Betty Macdonald, James Thurber and Dorothy Parker and *The Marx Brothers Scripts*. The horoscopes were drawn up by Linda Goodman and Barry Fantoni and an anonymous Chinese astrologer whose book I found in Covent Garden.

Picture Credits

(with thanks to David M. Robb Jr, The Tallulah Bankhead Society, Huntsville, Alabama)

Pg. 90	Courtesy of the National Portrait Gallery, Smithsonian Institution
Pg. 36, 44, 134	Courtesy Kobal
Pg. 66, 108	From the Rawls/Seawell collection, University of North Carolina
	All other pictures courtesy of Alabama Department of Archives and History, Montgomery, Alabama

Filmography

Her films are worth a look for their period charm and a window on a world purer, simpler and more black-and-white than our own. Sadly, none of them are available on video.

1918	Thirty A Week (silent)	1932	Make Me A Star
1918	When Men Betray (silent)	1932	Thunder Below
1919	The Trap (silent)	1943	Stage Door Canteen
1927	Woman's Law	1944	Lifeboat
1928	His House In Order	1945	A Royal Scandal
1931	The Cheat	1953	Main Street To Broadway
1931	My Sin	1965	Die! Die! My Darling!
1932	Tarnished Lady		(US: The Fanatic)
1932	Faithless	1966	The Daydreamer (voice only)

Notes

1. from *Kitchen Matters*, Bryony Lavery
2. from *Calling The Shots*, Bryony Lavery
3. ibid.
4. from the *Round The Horne Scripts*
5. from *Miss Tallulah Bankhead*, Lee Israel
6. from *Two Marias*, Bryony Lavery
7. from *Chines Horoscopes*, Barry Fantoni
8. from *Star Signs*, Linda Goodman
9. F. S. Fitzgerald
10. from *Kitchen Matters*, Bryony Lavery
11. from *Her Aching Heart*, Bryony Lavery
12. from *True and False: Heresy and Common Sense For The Actor*, David Mamet
13. from *More Light*, Bryony Lavery
14. from *The Oxford English Dictionary*
15. from *Breathing*, Michael Sky